The Fireship

Also by C. Northcote Parkinson

The Fireship

☆ ☆

C. Northcote Parkinson

HOUGHTON MIFFLIN COMPANY BOSTON

1975

For Antonia

☆ ☆

Contents

Chapter	1	The Partisan	9
	2	Mutiny	21
	3	The Court Martial	43
	4	The Tempest	65
	5	Camperdown	87
	6	The Aftermath	101
	7	The Fireship	115
	8	Fabius	137
	9	Revolt in Ireland	153
	10	The End of the Spitfire	171

Maps on pages 8, 42, 86, 170

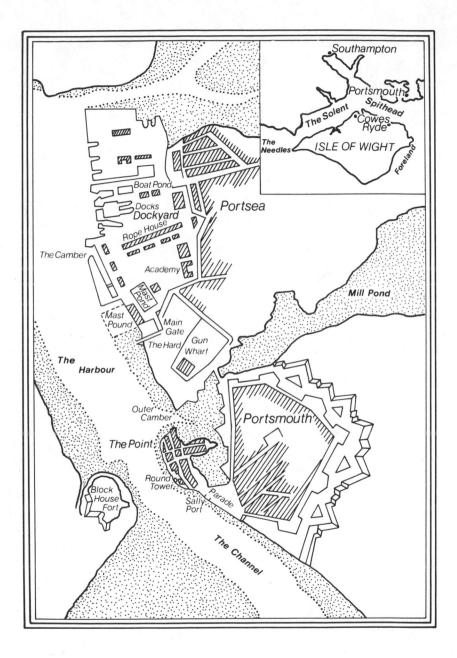

☆ ☆

The Partisan

THE FRIGATE *Medusa* was on her passage home from the Mediterranean and lay becalmed almost in sight of Falmouth. The sails flapped idle and useless beneath a dull grey sky. Captain Morris, not being the man to fret over a delay, instantly ordered an exercise in seamanship that would keep his men occupied. The foretopmast was to be sent down as if to be replaced and then sent up again and re-rigged, each watch to be timed in doing it. It meant stripping the mast down to the standing rigging below the foretop, an arduous task even in a flat calm. The men had of course done it all before, heaven knows how often, but it was one of the more popular crew exercises. When the order was given the seamen of the starboard watch worked methodically and well, leaving nothing undone and presenting a final result which would pass the first lieutenant's critical eye. The officer of the watch reported completion and a note was made of the exact time, only three seconds more than the previous record. Then the order was repeated and the seamen of the larboard watch fairly hurled themselves at the rigging. With more obvious and dramatic effort they raced through each phase and sweated to improve the timing. When the officer of the watch reported completion Rothery, the first lieutenant, timepiece in hand, was able to announce an improved time: one minute and twelve seconds quicker than the best previous result. The men of the larboard watch cheered and the captain said 'Well done!' A new record had been set up and the crew was presently piped to dinner. The only man who looked slightly unhappy was the boatswain, who had noticed one or two loose ends at the conclusion of the exercise. The sky brightened in the afternoon with a freshening westerly breeze. The sails filled, the bow wave gleamed white and the voyage was resumed, the frigate being under orders to report to the Commander-in-Chief at the Nore.

The two officers whose abilities and men had been tested that morning were very different in type. The larboard watch was led by John Meade, an active young man of a naval family, keen and well liked. Leading the starboard watch was Richard Delancey. His presence on board was somewhat accidental, a result of a raid on the Spanish coast. Wrecked on the Biscay Coast and imprisoned, Delancey had escaped with a handful of his crew, crossed Spain in disguise, ambushed a courier and obtained some vital information about the Spanish Admiral Langara's plans. During the rescue Lieutenant Halsted had been killed and Captain Morris filled the vacancy by appointing Delancey. Three results of this affair are worthy of note. Delancey's intelligence had proved correct: Admiral Langara did sail for Toulon, as predicted, with the object of joining his fleet to that of France. The British Mediterranean fleet, quite unequal to meeting this combined force, had been withdrawn from its station, many of its ships being given a defensive role based on British ports. The *Medusa* was one of these, being also due for a refit. As a result of the Léon skirmish Captain Morris had been offered the command of a ship-of-the-line, the *Bulwark* (74) on the Channel Station. His transfer to a bigger ship was somewhat overdue and mention of him in a gazette letter had reminded somebody at the Admiralty of his existence. He knew, on that homeward passage that his time in the *Medusa* was nearly finished.

Delancey knew it too. Soon after docking at Chatham the old

despairing routine of trying to get a posting would begin again. But what sort of posting did he want? He was completely without 'interest', that essential connection with influential people that was responsible for many a spectacular naval career. To gain promotion his only chance was to be made first lieutenant. If the ship to which he had been appointed were then to capture an enemy ship of equal or superior force, the captain would probably be knighted and he, as first lieutenant, would be promoted master and commander. But Delancey knew that few of the first lieutenants so promoted were actually given a command. They were given the rank as a compliment and then left on the beach, perhaps for years and often for good.

The *Medusa* made good time up Channel and dropped anchor at the Nore. After reporting to the flagship Morris was ordered to take his ship into Chatham. There she was found to be in a worse state of repair than even her carpenter had supposed. Timbers were rotten below the waterline and a whole section of her stern would have to be rebuilt. Captain Morris left the ship at this point, being posted to the *Bulwark*. Most of the *Medusa*'s crew were drafted to other ships, Rothery being left in command of the party that remained. Readily obtaining leave, the other officers went off to pester the Admiralty, write to their patrons and visit their homes. Delancey had neither patron nor home and came to spend much of his time round the dockyard itself. He knew something of the shipwright's art, having once had a shore appointment in America. This was his chance to learn more. He was also interested in the appearance of ships in dry dock, looking up at them from the dock floor. He made sketches from this unusual angle and convinced himself that some of them had artistic merit as well as professional accuracy. He was often on the quayside when a ship was warped in and stripped to her lower masts, her fighting tops showing strangely bulky against the sky. Coming to know Chatham Dockyard well, he used to foregather at the Golden

Cockerel with other officers who had nowhere to go, promoted boatswains and gunners who had little or no chance of further promotion, but who knew the Navy from a lifetime in the service. The group he joined in the evening was headed by old 'Crowbar' Crowley, who had fought under Sir Charles Saunders at Quebec and now held a minor dockyard appointment. He was usually supported by two other veterans, Lieutenant Wetherall and Dumbell, and by such officers as were passing through. On the third night old Wetherall reported that he'd heard the *Glatton* was soon to be back in the dockyard for alterations and repair. The others showed immediate interest and Delancey remembered her recent action against a French squadron. She was commanded by Captain Henry Trollope, and the affair had involved a remarkable disparity of force. He had forgotten the precise details until Wetherall reminded him.

'Trollope was on his way to join Admiral Duncan off Helvoetsluys. One evening he fell in with four French frigates, two ship corvettes, one brig corvette and a cutter. The odds against the *Glatton* must have been about six to one'.

'More like seven or eight to one,' Dumbell interrupted. 'The French Commodore's frigate was herself probably larger than the *Glatton*.'

'Well, she may have been at that. Anyway, there was a night action, beginning at pistol-shot range, and the French ships were so damaged that one of them sank soon afterwards in Flushing harbour. They fairly broke off the action and fled.'

'And the *Glatton*?' asked Delancey.

'She had only one man killed,' said Wetherall, 'Captain Strangeways of the Marines, who returned to his post after a tourniquet had been applied to his thigh, fainted from loss of blood and died soon after he was once more taken below. There were only a few wounded. Apart from her sails being cut to ribbons, the *Glatton* and her crew were little the worse.'

'What an extraordinary story!' Delancey exclaimed, calling

for another round of drinks. 'How was it possible?'

'I'll tell you, sir,' said old Crowley. 'The *Glatton* was one of nine East Indiamen bought last year from their owners and turned into men-of-war—'

'And damned bad ones at that!' growled Dumbell.

'Too narrow in the beam,' Crowley admitted, 'and with too little room for the recoil of the guns. Warships, however, they were to be and the *Glatton* of 1256 tons was to mount 56 cannon.'

'Making her something between a frigate and a ship of the line,' said Dumbell, 'and no damned use as either.'

'Be that as it may,' Crowley continued, 'Captain Trollope was given the command, the man who was captain of the *Rainbow* during the last war; the commander before that of the *Kite*, as clever an officer as you will find in the service. He proposed that the *Glatton* should be armed only with carronades—68-pounders on the lower deck, 32-pounders on the upper deck—with not a blessed long gun in the ship. The Navy Board accepted this plan—'

'While members of the Board of Ordnance nearly died of apoplexy,' added Wetherall.'

'And that is how she was armed in July. The French never knew what had hit them.'

The details about the *Glatton's* armament were new to Delancey. He began to do some sums on a scrap of paper and looked up after a few moments:

'The *Glatton* fires probably a 1540-lb broadside, more than that of a three-decker like the *Queen Charlotte* and enough to blow any opponent out of the water!'

'But, lookee,' said Dumbell, 'why don't we arm all our ships like that?'

'Because it would be lunacy,' replied Crowley. 'These carronades are short-range weapons. After the first encounter the enemy would not come within half a mile. Then we should be destroyed by long guns firing at long range, and we not able to reply.'

'There must be other difficulties,' said Delancey. 'The *Glatton* can have no room for the crew she needs. And how can these carronades be aimed? A 68-pounder must pretty well fill the port, having no room to traverse . . .'

'You are right, sir!' exclaimed Crowley, 'And that is the problem we shall have to solve when the *Glatton* is docked.'

'I look forward to seeing her,' said Delancey.

The group went on to talk about a subject much discussed at this time, the question of seamen's pay: the soldiers had been given a pay increase but there had been none for the Navy.

'There will be trouble over this,' said Dumbell, 'you mark my words. It's not merely that they need the money but the lads are asking why the sodgers should be treated better. Who have won the victories? We have! And who have the enemy managed to beat? The sodgers!' Here was a subject that would last them half the evening and Delancey presently excused himself. He reflected, however, that they were right about the seamen's pay. It was madness, he thought, to do so little for men on whom the government relied so much. Old Dumbell had been right about the possibility of mutiny. It looked different, he supposed, from the Minister's point of view, with so many other financial demands to meet, but the sailors had a case. He went back to the *Medusa* in thoughtful mood.

When the *Glatton* dropped anchor at the Nore Delancey was among those who were watching. She was an ungainly ship, still very much the Indiaman, and looked ugly beside the other men-of-war. When she warped into the graving dock he was again on the quayside and soon found an excuse for going on board. He had some slight acquaintance with Captain Trollope, going back to the previous war, but had no reason to suppose that the captain would remember him. The matter was not put to the test, however, for Trollope was not there. He had posted to London from Sheerness and left the *Glatton* under the temporary command of her keenly efficient second lieutenant, Mr Alexander Grant. Delancey was allowed on board and studied the various problems created by the ship's freak armament. He asked about the lower-deck carronades' lack of traverse.

'Oh, that's the least of it,' said Grant with a touch of impatience. 'At the range we opened fire that was of no consequence. Our trouble began with having thirty men too few for the guns we mount. Our troubles ended—so far as our recent action was concerned—with the muzzle blast scorching the timber. Come and see for yourself!'

On the *Glatton*'s lower deck, stripped as she was for docking, it was difficult to imagine the ship in action. In the gloomy half light the deck space was cluttered with carpenters' gear and a blacksmith's forge. The workmen had ended their efforts for the day but several were still there, whistling as they prepared to go home. Grant pointed to various marks of burning.

'It did no real damage but the framework round each port will have to be rebuilt.'

'It would not appear, sir, that you suffered much from the enemy's shot.'

'We suffered amazingly little and our few losses were due to long-range fire from a confounded brig and a cutter. The French frigates were so taken by surprise that they fired at random or not at all.'

'I should suppose that your men are in good heart, following such a victory?'

'That is partly true but they won no prize money.'

'Could they expect any, fighting at such odds? Why, if you had taken a prize the French Commodore would have shot himself after signing his report and before the court-martial could assemble.'

'Yes, but one of their frigates sank afterwards in harbour. We claimed head-money for that and it was disallowed. It was said that she would be floated again.'

'I expect she will but I would guess that Captain Trollope is still arguing about it at the Admiralty.'

'He is at the Admiralty, right enough, but the argument is over the ship's armament. The Ordnance Board want to change everything—never having approved it in the first place—and the captain likes it the way it is, just as he planned it.'

'On which side, sir, are you placing your bet?'

'Well, they will refer the question to a committee, meeting here next month, and my guess is that the captain will have his way. He usually does!'

Trollope returned from London before the end of the month and Delancey went to call on him at his lodgings ashore in Chatham. He turned out to be very much what Delancey had remembered—a slim, restless man with piercing eyes, rapid in his speech and quick to understand. He had probably no recollection of having met Delancey before but he showed interest at once when gunnery was mentioned and specifically the problem posed by a large carronade in a small gun-port. Delancey explained his interest and added that he had served ashore during the siege of Gibraltar.

'And may I ask,' said Trollope, 'whether that experience sheds light on the present problem?'

'Possibly, sir. The Spanish artillerymen manning their floating batteries had to fire through wooden embrasures ten foot thick. To guard against muzzle flash they lined the embrasures with sheet tin. I think that is a practicable method of protecting the timber.'

'How did you come to know about it?'

'I reconnoitred the batteries, sir, while they were still under construction.'

Before the meeting broke up, Trollope had come to the conclusion that Delancey was a very promising officer. They supped together that night and parted with expressions of mutual esteem.

It was a lucky chance that brought Trollope and Delancey together. Trollope had an original mind and admitted to having little use for the concepts of seamanship and discipline which were the accepted gospel on board the *Medusa*. He questioned some hallowed traditions and shook some cherished beliefs. He was apt to ask why in circumstances which seemed to call rather for agreement and unanimity. The result, moreover, of his recent victory was to place him in a strong position, commended by his sovereign and idolised by the public. He saw in Delancey a man of his own kind, one more interested in gunnery than in ceremonial; a man who might be something of an intellectual, something of a dreamer, more absent-minded than an ideal officer should be, and yet clearly a man of action and courage, a useful man in a desperate situation. Suppressing any doubts he may have felt, Trollope made his decision. When assured of Delancey's agreement to the plan, he proposed to the Commander-in-Chief at the Nore (Vice-Admiral Buckner) that Delancey should be posted second, under Alexander Grant, to the *Glatton*. Captain Morris agreed very readily and the appointment was approved by the Admiralty in December, 1796. With Grant on leave it fell to Delancey to attend the committee meeting which would decide the vexed question of the *Glatton's* armament. It was held in January, 1797.

A cold and clammy mist lay that day over the dockyard, lower masts being barely visible, the ships themselves no more than a blur in the fog. Lamps were still lit on the coaches which had just entered the dockyard and the coachmen were stamping to warm their feet outside the Commissioner's house. As the recent arrivals made their way down to the quayside, top-coated and muffled, the noise of hammering grew louder. Guided more by this noise than by anything they could see, they presently found themselves at the foot of a gangway. It led to the *Glatton*, which was still in dock for repair, and they were met on deck by a guide who turned out to be a foreman shipbuilder. He led them aft to the captain's day cabin, lit by lanterns and warmed by a portable stove. The floor space was partly occupied by a squat and powerful piece of ordnance but there was still room for a borrowed table and a few ill-assorted chairs. The noise of hammering was much louder now—the carpenters seemed to be at work somewhere amidships—and the Commissioner did the honours in dumb show, waving the others to their seats and encouraging them to shed their topcoats and cloaks. He next sent the foreman forward and the hammering presently ceased. The sound of a saw could still be heard in the distance and the noise of a pair of draught horses being led along the quayside. The Commissioner now called the meeting to order and all present took their seats round the table.

'It is my privilege, gentlemen, to bid you welcome to His Majesty's Dockyard at Sheerness. Some or all of you are known, to each other but I will name each of you severally for the benefit of my clerk, Mr Fairhall, who will be recording what we decide. We have present, then, Captain Trollope who commands this ship, Captain White of the Navy Board, Mr Lucas of the Navy Board, Mr Rodgers of the Board of Ordnance and, finally, Mr Burrows of this Dockyard. Our task is to consider and recommend the ordnance to be mounted on board this vessel, His Majesty's ship *Glatton* of 56 guns and measuring 1256 tons. She is one of nine ships bought last year from the East India Company. These former Indiamen, built for commerce, differ in design from men-of-war built for their purpose. They are narrower in the beam with less room for the recoil of ordnance. For that and for other reasons it was decided to arm them with 18-pounder cannon on the upper deck and 32-pounder carronades on the lower deck. Captain Trollope proposed, however, that the *Glatton* should mount 68-

pounder carronades (not 32-pounders) on the lower deck and 32-pounder carronades on the upper deck. This plan was accepted and the *Glatton* fought a successful engagement in July last year. The Ordnance Board feel, however, that the ships should be rearmed as originally laid down. I thought it proper that we should meet on board the *Glatton* and have before us a 68-pounder carronade. I call on Mr Rodgers to tell us what he has in mind.'

'I am vastly obliged to you, Sir James, and will strive to avoid detaining you longer than is necessary for our purpose. The carronade was invented towards the conclusion of the last war by Mr Gascoigne of the Carron Ironworks near Falkirk in Scotland. It is, as I need hardly say, a shorter and lighter version of the carriage gun, firing a heavier projectile at a shorter range, recoiling on a slide and manned by a smaller crew. It came into general use in 1779 and its effectiveness was first proved in the action between the *Flora*, frigate, and the French ship *Nymphe*. The question was then asked whether a ship might not be armed with carronades alone. The *Rainbow* was so armed as an experiment in March, 1782, and Captain Trollope was given the command. We have no proof that this experiment was a success.'

'How can you say that?' asked Captain White, 'Captain Trollope captured the *Hébé*—and what a valuable prize that was! All our heavy frigates today are copies of the *Hébé*—a beautiful ship if ever there was one!'

'We all know that!' snapped Rodgers, 'But her capture proved nothing. She surrendered without a fight.'

'She surrendered,' said Trollope with emphasis, 'as soon as her captain knew the calibre of the guns he had to face. Now we have repeated the experiment, arming the *Glatton* in the same way and with much the same result. A whole French squadron fled from a single ship!'

'It was a night action,' Rodgers objected, 'and the French

had no prior information about their opponent. The whole French navy will be warned by now in a circular issued by their Minister of Marine.'

There was an acrimonious discussion and Delancey admired the adroit way in which Captain Trollope dealt with the opposition, winning over Lucas and Burrows and isolating Rodgers from the rest. Twenty minutes later the question of muzzle flash was raised and Trollope promptly turned to Delancey for support. For his part, Delancey decided that a junior officer should be brief.

'This problem was encountered, Sir Henry, by the Spanish when fitting out their floating batteries at the siege of Gibraltar. They solved it by lining their gun ports with sheet tin.'

'That did not save them,' said Rodgers.

'But neither were they burnt, sir, by sparks from their own gun muzzles.' There was some laughter at this, but to Delancey's surprise there was no further talk about muzzle flash—perhaps because tin was thought too expensive—and a disagreement arose over the carronades' tendency to overturn after firing. Sir Henry clearly thought that the discussion had continued long enough.

'There are problems,' he admitted, 'but we think—Mr Burrows and I—that we can solve them. On that assumption, may I take it that we have agreed, by a majority, to the *Glatton* being armed as at present until we receive further direction?'

Mr Rodgers frowned and shook his head but the others murmured their agreement and the Commissioner then adjourned the meeting. Leading the way back to his house and fireside, he reflected that there was this to be said for meeting on board the *Glatton*: the cold had led to a relatively quick decision.

☆ ☆

Mutiny

IN APRIL, 1797, the *Glatton* was at the buoy of the Nore, having come out of dock in February. She had been re-rigged since then, shipping the same crew as before, and had been in the Thames estuary for what we should now describe as gunnery trials. Returning to the Nore, Captain Trollope reported to Admiral Buckner that the trials had been successful, that the guns handled well as now mounted, that the various alterations had answered their purpose and that the ship was ready for active service. In response to this report Buckner sent for him aboard the flagship and told him in strict confidence, that the Channel Fleet had mutinied at Spithead. This astounding news had come that morning and would be in tomorrow's newspapers. The *Glatton* was to sail at once for the Dutch coast, incidentally carrying the news to Admiral Duncan.

'The mutiny is likely to spread,' explained Buckner, 'but crews actually at sea will at least be spared the bad example. I am ordering every ship to sea that is ready to sail.'

Captain Trollope needed no further urging and had the *Glatton* under way before the news of the mutiny had become public. Sending for his first lieutenant, he explained the situation. 'We shall need to be on our guard, Mr Grant,' he concluded. Having said that, he reflected that the *Glatton* was exceptionally well officered and manned. There might be some grumblers aboard—and Grant had said that there were—but most of the men were loyal enough. They had fought an entire French squadron, wrecking their opponents by gunfire and being cheered when they came ashore. Their officers were considerate and fair, everything possible was done for their comfort and even the boatswain was popular. Sometimes a new member of the crew would say 'Our Number One is no fiery dragon with his "Pray do this, my lads," and "Be so good as to belay that."' He would be put right in an instant, however, by the older seamen who would say: 'When Alex Grant goes into action, mate, you stand from under!' When Delancey was told the news he was similarly confident that the *Glatton* would be the last ship to mutiny. The government had made an appalling blunder over pay but he supposed it would be put right. As for the *Glatton*, the trouble with the ex-Indiaman was that she was betwixt and between, neither a frigate nor fit to take her place in the line of battle. Her crew had been unlucky over prize-money, there could be no doubt about that.

Delancey pondered these thoughts as he stood the morning watch, pacing the quarterdeck as the *Glatton* left the Thames estuary astern. The moon had set, the night was dark, the weather was fine and there was just a hint of light to the eastward, a forerunner of daybreak. From the foretop came the hail 'A strange sail on the starboard bow!' Delancey focussed his night glass and could just distinguish a distant silhouette. He handed the glass to a midshipman, young Harker, and told him to take it to the foretop-masthead. 'See what you make of her.'

The boy reached the deck again in five minutes. 'A ship-rigged merchantman, sir, heading this way!'

'How big?'

The boy hesitated and then replied 'About the same size as a smaller West Indiaman, sir.'

Taking the glass again, Delancey focussed it again. Why was the stranger not sailing in convoy? Perhaps she carried letters of marque. But even so. . . . He turned again to the youngster.

'My compliments to the captain. A strange ship in sight.' The
Glatton was close-hauled, the other ship had a following wind
and the distance between them was lessening fairly quickly.
They would be within hail in about an hour.

Captain Trollope came on deck with his own night glass and
focussed in the direction which Delancey indicated. 'Over 500
tons, maybe 600, English built but with something odd about
the sails; steering as if she wanted to intercept us. What do you
make of her?'

'Could be a French privateer.'

'What—off the Gunfleet?'

'I see what you mean. But it still makes no sense. Clear for
action in half an hour.'

Captain Trollope had gone again, probably to shave, and
Delancey resumed his pacing of the quarterdeck. No British
merchantman would go anywhere near a man-of-war, for fear
of the press-gang. No French merchant man would go anywhere near the Thames estuary. But the *Glatton* had begun life
as an East Indiaman and it was just possible that a privateer
might see her as a possible prey. It argued a captain of exceptional daring but there might be someone out of St Malo with
that much enterprise, sailing a captured ship which might not
seem too out of place in English waters. After the necessary
lapse of time he called out 'Clear for action!' Within about a
minute the drum was beating and the watch below was turning
out. There was the usual bustle and turmoil, ending with the
decks cleared and the guns manned. Grant presently reported
to the captain that the crew were at quarters and the guns run
out. It was still fairly dark, with the strange ship almost within
range.

'Make the night recognition signal,' ordered Captain Trollope, and some lanterns were hoisted in the pattern prescribed.
There was no reply, which ruled out the possibility of the other
ship being a British man-of-war. Even a British merchantman

would have made some sort of reply. She might, of course, be under a neutral flag, and it was this possibility which suggested caution. 'Light a flare!' was the next order and the resulting effect was to illuminate the other ship for perhaps half a minute. She was nearly as large as the *Glatton* and her ports were open, her guns manned. She was presumably French or she would not be offering battle, but she did not appear to be a national frigate. If she were a privateer, however, her commander must be out of his mind. Given a ship with a more normal armament, Trollope would at this stage have tried the range, firing a shot across the stranger's bows. But he had only short-range weapons and would do nothing except at close quarters. 'Another flare!' he ordered and had glimpsed the tricolour being hoisted before it was dark again. A few moments later the French ship fired her broadside and then tacked so as to place herself on the same course as the *Glatton*, firing her other broadside as she did so. Trollope then closed the range to little more than pistol shot, receiving another ineffective broadside before he finally gave the order to open fire. The deck reeled under him as the carronades went off together.

Delancey's post was on the lower deck and this was the first time he had seen the 68-pounder carronades in action. He had learnt the drill for the carronade and its smaller crew and could see that the *Glatton*'s men were steady under fire and unlikely to make a mistake. Their difficulty was with the weight of the shot and he doubted whether they could keep up the maximum rate of fire for long. He realised, however, that the *Glatton*'s broadside must have an unimaginable impact. What with smoke and darkness there was little to be seen but he could hear the crash as shot went through their opponent's hull. The French cannon must have been quite small and few of their shot seemed to penetrate. 'Steady, boys,' he shouted, 'cartridge seam downwards and ram well home. Watch your target and aim before you fire.' The noise was deafening and the acrid smell of expended gunpowder was worse than he had known in any other ship. But more powder was being burnt, of course. As he went along the battery he made the after guns train forward, the forward guns aft, concentrating the fire on the enemy ship's waist.

Before the next broadside, however, a midshipman dashed up to him saluting and said, 'Captain's compliments, sir, and he desires you to cease fire.'

Delancey shouted 'Cease fire!' and the cry was taken up along the deck. 'Stand by your guns!' was the next order and each gun crew stood ready to fire again at the word of command. The smoke drifted away and Delancey could see their opponent, still on their beam and now silent. She must have hauled down her colours after receiving three broadsides.

Another boy appeared beside him. 'Captain's compliments, sir, and will you take possession of the prize?' Delancey ran to fetch his cloak, leaving a master's mate in command of the battery.

When Delancey came on deck, a few minutes later, the carpenter was already examining the longboat and the boatswain was already checking her gear. Delancey found the captain and first lieutenant on the quarterdeck, looking across at the prize, now plainly visible in the growing light. She was hove to with her masts all standing and there was little visible damage above the hammock nettings. Between her gun ports, however, there were gaping holes and planks torn apart. Several of her ports were empty and Delancey could just hear the creaking sound of her pumps at work.

'Take possession, Mr Delancey, and report on her damage and casualties.'

'Aye, aye, sir. May I take the carpenter with me?'

'Yes, do that. Send her officers back in the boat and signal when you are ready to proceed. I mean to take her into Yarmouth.'

'Congratulations, sir, on taking a valuable prize.'

'Let's hope she is valuable. I can't make out what she is or what her master thought he was doing.'

The longboat was lowered into the water and the boat's crew assembled, armed with muskets and bayonets. Into the stern-sheets went John Huntley, fourth lieutenant and Robert Appleby, midshipman. Delancey came last and the boat pushed off. In ten minutes time he was on the deck of the prize, confronted by an agitated Frenchman who offered his sword. Delancey accepted it, handing it to a petty officer. The French-man then reported that his ship was the *Confiance*, privateer, out of Cherbourg, and that his own name was Dufossey. The ship had previously been the *Sheldrake* out of London.

'Why were you in the Thames Estuary?'

'I had learnt that the British seamen had all mutinied, and that your men-of-war are in port. I hoped that my ship would pass as British.'

'How did you hear of the mutiny?'

'From a fishing boat off the Isle of Wight.'

'And why did you attack us?'

'I took you for an Indiaman.'

'So now you know the difference.'

'But your cannon are not those of an ordinary man-of-war. We thought the end of the world had come!'

'The end of your cruise, anyway. Now, captain, I want you and your officers to go to H.M. Ship *Glatton* as prisoners of war. I give you ten minutes to collect your gear. In the meanwhile, order your men to surrender all small arms, bringing them here. And tell your carpenter to report to me at once.'

Delancey's fluent French was a help on such an occasion. With the *Glatton*'s carpenters he made a quick inspection be-tween decks, seeing the tremendous havoc done by the 68-pounder shot. Several guns had been dismounted and one, opposite the after hatch, had completely disappeared. Then he returned to the entry port and saw the French officers over the side. 'I think the ship is badly damaged,' said the captain when they parted, and Delancey agreed with a nod. 'Come back for the small arms,' he ordered the coxswain. Then he turned to meet Charrier, the French carpenter, saying quickly 'Show me!'

Charrier led the way, followed by Delancey and the *Glatton*'s carpenter, Jenkins. On the main deck Charrier paused by the after hatch and explained that a gun had been hit and had fallen into the hold. 'It looks bad,' he explained with a grimace.

Delancey guessed at once how bad it might be. A ship's hull is designed to resist pressure from the outside and can stand up to a fair amount of buffeting. A blow from the inside is a different matter, tending to loosen the fastenings, and such a concussion near the keel is worst of all, being difficult of access. They went down to the hold, where there was already more than a foot of water. Had the gun, the French equivalent of a 9-pounder, pitched on the planking it would probably have gone through it, sinking the ship outright. Its fall had been partly broken by a wooden box but the box had been empty and the planks below had started. Two carpenter's mates had been trying to patch the leak but their efforts had failed. Delancey sent one of them on deck, telling him to sound the well every ten minutes. Then Charrier took him to see three other leaks. One, between wind and water, had been patched from the outside and was admitting no more than a trickle. Another, below the water line, had been stuffed with canvas and nailed up with spare timber. It would probably hold in fine weather, at least for an hour or two. The third was in the bows, where it was quite inaccessible. It might have been small at first but there was an audible intake which would presumably enlarge the hole.

There was much other damage and the French had lost eleven men killed and twenty-three wounded. They had two pumps working and were plainly doing their best. Going on deck, Delancey asked the carpenter's mate whether the leaks had gained over the last ten minutes. They had, he was told, by seven inches. He ordered the French boatswain to organise a chain of buckets at the main hatch.

Someone found a sheet of paper and Delancey knelt at a skylight with a stub of pencil which he found in his pocket. With pumps working the ship was leaking at the rate of 3' 6" an hour and would sink in about three hours' time. The chain of buckets might gain another half hour. With a fresh easterly wind a waterlogged ship would take at least ten hours to reach Yarmouth. So that was hopeless. What about Harwich? Two hours and a half? It would be a damn close thing. If he fothered a sail under the ship's bottom he might slow down the leak but he would lose time in doing it. The calculation finished, he saw that the longboat was returning and that Captain Trollope was coming aboard. A discussion followed, with both carpenters present, while Huntley supervised the loading of the small arms into the boat. Delancey submitted his figures and Trollope glanced at them. Then he made a quick decision.

'To save this ship is impossible. You, Mr Delancey, will be responsible for sinking her. Tell the French to lower all boats and abandon ship. I shall land all prisoners at Harwich before going on to Yarmouth. I want to be underway in thirty minutes.' He went back to his own ship which he brought nearer to the prize.

Delancey meanwhile told the French to quit the pumps and collect their belongings. He ordered Huntley to rig one of the cannon so as to aim into the hold, with gun's crew ready and ammunition at hand. He told young Appleby to see whether any of the stores were worth saving, especially the wine. He told the French boatswain to lower all boats and have them ready to man. After twenty minutes of furious activity Delancey told the gun's crew to fire through the ship's bottom and then again, to make sure. The French needed no other hint and were soon tumbling into their boats. Within the half hour Delancey was on his way back to the *Glatton*, the longboat towing a string of barrels and loaded with French cabin stores. The *Confiance* sank as the *Glatton* made sail again. Delancey and his men had earned a word of commendation from the captain. What they had not earned was prize-money.

This last fact had not escaped the notice of the ship's grumblers; Mick Donovan and Paddy O'Keefe, ordinary seamen, Steve Collins, captain of the head, Sam Cox, able seaman and Tom Batley, landsman and sea lawyer. Batley had been a parish clerk in Suffolk. There had been a question about some money missing from the poor-box, a further question about a pregnant girl in the workhouse, and Tom left in a hurry for London. He ended as the spokesman, if not the actual leader, of the malcontents on board an otherwise happy ship. He had much to say at the mess table on the subject of prize-money.

'We'll get none aboard the *Glatton*,' replied O'Leary. 'She sails like a worn out collier.'

'There's one thing about her worse than that,' argued Collins. 'The captain has no knighthood.'

'What harm is there in that?' asked Sam Cox.

'Why, don't you know, you ignorant lubber?' asked Collins. 'A captain who wants a knighthood will fight bigger French ships until he gets it. Damn the killed or wounded—all he wants is his name in the *Gazette*. Once he has it he begins to count the enemy gun-ports.'

After landing the prisoners and calling at Yarmouth, the *Glatton* joined Admiral Duncan's flag on the Dutch coast. Trollope brought with him the first news of the mutiny at Spithead and was told to keep it to himself. The precaution was a wise one but the news, in the nature of things, could not be suppressed for long. In the meanwhile, Admiral Duncan continued to blockade the enemy coast.

For week after week, for month after month, the North Sea
Fleet had cruised off the Texel, occasionally taking refuge in
Yarmouth Roads when there was a westerly gale. Now the *Glatton* fell in with the same routine and her crew resigned themselves to the same monotony of work. Two days after she joined
there was, however, a break in the monotony. There had been a
thick mist in the early morning which presently vanished in the
warm sunlight, revealing quite suddenly a small brig on the
flagship's weather quarter. She seemed to have come from
nowhere but her function was easy to guess and any doubt
about it was ended by a signal. The mail had come. A boat from
each ship rowed off to collect it and within the hour a bundle of
letters and packets had been placed on the wardroom table.
Only three letters were addressed to Delancey, two bills and a
receipt, but Pringle received a newspaper and presently called
out to the others, 'Listen to this! The seamen's petition is given
in full but this is the key paragraph:

> 'We profess ourselves as loyal to our sovereign, and zea-
> lous, in the defence of our country, as the army or militia can
> be, and esteem ourselves equally entitled to his Majesty's
> munificence: therefore with jealousy we behold their pay
> augmented . . . while we remain neglected.'

'They have much right on their side and I can't think how the
ministers could agree to favour the army in this way.'
Listening to this, Delancey could imagine what was being
said on the lower deck. And the mischief was that the newspapers, quoting the words of the petition, gave no hint of any
response from the Admiralty. For all the seamen could know
the demands of the Channel Fleet were going to be rejected.
Delancey could not believe that a refusal was possible but
wished devoutly that the newspapers had contained some hint
of an expected settlement.
Later in the day Captain Trollope addressed the whole crew,

giving them the facts of the mutiny as known to him and adding, 'The conduct of the seamen at Spithead has been very wrong and most unwise. I think it certain, nevertheless, that their reasonable demands will be met and that you will all have better pay before long. Be patient until we have further news. Set a good example rather than choose to follow a bad one. Here, off the Texel, we are in sight of the enemy. The Dutch have 18 sail of the line with 22 frigates and sloops and there are 4,000 French troops ready to embark. We do not know their plans but we know what will happen to our homes, our wives and children, if the French are suffered to land in England. We are here to prevent them and we could have no better leader than Admiral Duncan. We shall never allow the enemy to pass.' The men dispersed, but without cheering, and the officers exchanged some anxious looks.

The next westerly gale brought the North Sea Fleet back to Yarmouth where it promptly mutinied, the only ships still loyal being the *Venerable* (Duncan's flagship) and the *Adamant* (Vice-Admiral Onslow). The *Glatton* mutinied still sooner, quitting the fleet before Yarmouth was even reached. Delancey first knew of it when shaken in his cot by a midshipman.

'On deck, sir, quickly! The seamen have mutinied!'

Delancey turned out in an instant, pulled on his breeches and jacket, thrust his feet into sea boots and grabbed his sword. At the last minute he pocketed a pistol, half expecting to find himself in hand-to-hand conflict. The wardroom, however, was oddly quiet, the other officers being assembled there, all hastily dressed and armed.

'The captain is on deck,' explained Grant, 'and has ordered us to meet him here.' A minute later Captain Trollope entered quickly, accompanied by Anderson, the marine subaltern. He sat down at the head of the table with his face in his hands. When he looked up the others could see that he was white and drawn, looking older and tired.

'I have to tell you, gentlemen, that the men have mutinied. They have broken into several of the arms chests and are provided with weapons and ammunition. They have placed their own sentries on the magazine. There has been no violence, just a demand that I sail for Spithead. I have told them that their conduct is lunacy. I have urged them to return to their duty but nothing I say seems to have any effect. Mr Huntley is on deck as officer of the watch but the men will obey no orders save such as will take them to Spithead. We are now on our way there, having deserted our Admiral's flag. Sit down, gentlemen, and give me your advice. I have to decide on a plan.'

The officers sat round the table, their only light coming from a single lantern. Two other lanterns were now brought in, shedding some pale illumination on a row of anxious and puzzled faces.

'This is a sad moment for me,' said Captain Trollope wearily; 'I have no authority in my own ship. I have, seemingly, two alternatives. I can call on the marines to crush the mutiny, assisted by such of the seamen as can be relied upon. Or else I can let the men have their way for the time being and deal with the ringleaders later on. I am assuming, you see, that I have these alternatives, but you may tell me that I haven't. Have I the force to regain control of the ship? Mr Grant?'

'Yes, sir. I think you have. The seamen are loyal, in the main; of this I am sure. The mutiny is caused by a very few bad characters—by men known to me as having had a bad influence all along. Put them in irons and the rest will return to their duty.'

'Thank you, Mr Grant. Do you agree with that, Mr Delancey?'

'No, sir. I should agree with Mr Grant if we were alone in this. If I am not mistaken, however, we have to deal with the fleet as a whole. The men are looking to the other ships for support, and that, I take it, is why they insist on going to Spithead.'

'Thank you, Mr Delancey. Well, Captain Mitchell, can we

rely on the marines?'

'We could have relied on them if the sailors had used violence, threatening you, sir, or the other officers. But there has been none of that. The seamen want higher pay but so do the marines. They have not disobeyed me yet but I would rather not risk an order that *might* be disobeyed. I don't think we can use the marines against the sailors.'

'Mr Pringle?'

'Our men are mostly loyal, as Mr Grant says, but they have a grievance about prize-money. They defeated the enemy in an engagement which will go down in history but went unrewarded afterwards. Then came our capture of the *Confiance*, another disappointment. This has caused bad feeling and our sea lawyers have made the most of it.'

'Thank you. Dr Mackenzie?'

'Frankly, sir, I think the men have been poorly treated in the matter of pay. That is no excuse for mutiny but I cannot but feel a measure of sympathy for them. I believe, moreover, that they will have the public on their side. Once their pay is improved they will return to their duty but they want to see the actual money. Promises from the Admiralty will not be enough.'

'Thank you, Dr Mackenzie. Anyone else? Well, I agree with you, Dr Mackenzie, about the seamen's pay. Higher wages will probably be agreed but it will take time. God knows what mischief there will be in the meanwhile. As for me, I have no choice. We must go to Spithead, where we shall find ourselves among other ships in a state of mutiny. Short of blowing the ship up, there is nothing else I can do.'

The passage to Spithead took nearly ten days, with southwesterly winds reaching gale force from time to time. Not the handiest of ships at any time, the *Glatton* was driven back repeatedly, losing on one day all the distance she had made the day before. By the time she dropped anchor at Spithead the mutiny, for the Channel Fleet, was over. The *Glatton*, flying the red flag of mutiny, looked conspicuous at anchor among the other ships, each by now flying her proper ensign. No officer made any comment on this but the red flag came down at sunset and was never hoisted again. As Captain Trollope soon learnt, the mutiny had been finally ended by summoning Lord Howe back from retirement. It had been the last great effort of his long career, beginning with a patient round of negotiations and ending with an even more exhausting visit to each ship in turn. There was loyal cheering in the end and a general return to duty, the seamen's chief demands having been met. On the day following their arrival at Spithead (a Sunday) the *Glatton*'s men were allowed to visit other ships and many of them did so, learning how the mutiny had come to an end. It had finished, they were told, on May 14th when the seamen's delegates, leaders of the mutiny and ripe (as many would have said) for a noose at the yardarm, had ended a day of rejoicing by having dinner with Lord Howe himself. There had been an amnesty with forgiveness for all. It did not apply, however, to ships like the *Glatton* which were still in a state of mutiny after the royal pardon had been issued. Talking with seamen on board the other ships the *Glatton* mutineers came to feel their isolation and sense the danger in which they stood.

The *Glatton* had come to Spithead owing to her mutineers' insistence but had no business there in the ordinary way. It was inevitable, therefore, that the Port Admiral should order Captain Trollope to the Nore. He knew that the ships there were in a state of mutiny but assumed that they would soon follow the example set by the Channel Fleet. The *Glatton*'s men might be a good influence and, apart from that, it was only at the Nore or at Chatham that they could expect to be paid. On the day before the ship was to sail, the spokesman of the mutineers—Batley, the sea-lawyer—came to Mr Pringle and asked whether the captain would receive a deputation from the crew. He was presently told that the captain would see the deputation in an hour's time. When the appointed time came, some eleven seamen shuffled into the captain's day cabin where Captain Trollope confronted them at his desk with the first lieutenant at his elbow and Dixon, the Master-at-Arms, in the immediate background.

'Well, my men, what can I do for you?' asked the captain. Stepping forward a pace, Batley explained that he had been authorised to speak for the rest.

'We have agreed, sir, to say how sorry we are for all that has happened. We remain loyal to the King and are ready to sail against his enemies. So far as we are concerned, the mutiny is over and we are returning to duty. We have never had anything but respect and affection for you, sir, and for our officers, and we hope to be forgiven for all we have done wrong.'

'Well, men, I think you are behaving very sensibly. The mutiny is over, as you could see for yourselves, and all your justified complaints have been answered. If you return to duty now I don't doubt that Admiral Duncan will forget the content of my previous report.'

'Thank you, sir,' said Batley, 'but are we covered by the royal pardon?'

'Strictly speaking, you are not. You have been in a state of mutiny *after* the pardon was issued. But I don't doubt that a lenient view will be taken.'

'Our lives are at stake, sir.'

'The safety of the whole kingdom is at stake. Anyway, I accept your submission and return to duty. My first order to you is to surrender all weapons to the Master-at-Arms.'

'We daren't do that, sir—not until we are sure about the pardon.'

'Then you are still in a state of mutiny and stand in greater danger than ever.'

'I'm sorry, sir. I'll discuss the matter with these other delegates and then we'll explain the situation to the crew. I don't think they'll disarm while they are in doubt about the pardon. In every other way we'll obey orders, sir.'

The captain remonstrated in vain, finally dismissing the deputation and turning in disgust to the first lieutenant.

'I believed for a moment that we had finished with this nonsense. We are still, however, at a deadlock.'

'I'll confess, sir,' said Grant tensely, 'that I'm out of patience with these fools. If I had Batley in irons the rest would give us no trouble.'

'What's your opinion, Master-at-Arms?' asked the captain.

'Well, sir, I wouldn't say that Batley was the real leader. He does the talking but the men to watch are Donovan and Collins—begging your pardon, sir. Cox is the bully the others are afraid of—Batley more than the rest, I reckon. Collins has a deal of influence, even over Cox. Of course we should have Batley in the bilboes while we are about it. But he talks more than he does.'

'I know, sir,' said Grant, 'that some of the officers agree with the Master-at-Arms over this. I think myself that Batley is dangerous. There is something so damned insolent about the fellow, nothing definite, nothing against the Articles of War, but a hidden defiance. We'll see him swing yet.'

'I'll have no action now which would trigger off another and worse mutiny. Send for Mr Delancey, though, I should like to have his opinion.' Grant passed the word and there was a little more discussion. Then Delancey reported and Captain Trollope told him what had happened.

'What do you think, Mr Delancey? Should we arrest the ringleaders now?'

'I doubt if that would be wise, sir. They have so far been moderate and they have the men's support. The time to take action, I submit, will be when they go too far. Then we shall have the crew on our side.'

'Will they go too far?'

'I think they will. The mutiny at the Nore is likely to be more violent. If they follow the example of the other ships there our men will turn against them.'

'But what makes you believe that things will be worse at the Nore?'

'Two things, sir. The worst recruits we have, my Lord Mayor's men, the overflow from Newgate, the King's hard bargain and the men with some education, are all sent down the river from London and join the ships at Chatham or Sheerness. And then, a mutinous fleet at the Nore is in a position to blockade the capital and so drive a harder bargain than a fleet based on Portsmouth. Batley and his friends may turn to violence when they know what is happening at the Nore. They may be still more violent when they hear that the mutiny has been suppressed and that their day is over.'

'But the suppression of a mutiny among those bad characters may not be easy.'

'Not easy, sir. But the government has the whip hand. It can cut off the ship's supply of food and water.'

'Very true, Mr Delancey. So you think we should wait?'

'Yes, sir.'

It was Delancey's advice that prevailed and Grant could hardly hide his impatience. He had his own ideas about how mutineers should be treated. What he had failed to realise was the extent to which Captain Trollope's career hung in the balance. There were officers whose men had mutinied and who might never have another command. Sir John Colpoys was almost certainly one of them. There were other officers, like Bligh, who saw active service again but who were still remembered for the wrong reason. Trollope's career had been one, by contrast, of continual success. He was a brilliant officer, as everyone knew, and could hardly fail to complete a distinguished career. But what if his crew mutinied and put him ashore? A dozen other reputations had collapsed but where was the consolation in that? Trollope was a man who had never failed. One single mishap now could reduce him to the level of those who had done pretty well on the whole and who might end, with luck, as a rear-admiral in a shore appointment. He was now at the height of his powers, a coming man, restless with energy and yet with plenty of experience behind him. To one so intensely ambitious the thought of seeing his career wrecked by a handful of nonentities and petty criminals was too painful to contemplate. As ambitious himself, although with far poorer prospects, Delancey had some insight into Trollope's attitude towards the mutineers. Grant felt the strain differently, horrified at the situation and eager to restore discipline. There was friction between them in the wardroom, with words exchanged rather curtly. Fully aware of these tensions, Trollope would have liked to end them by taking the ship into battle. There was no immediate chance of that but it was something, at least, to take the ship to sea.

The *Glatton* sailed next day but the breeze veered nor'westerly before the *Glatton* reached the North Foreland. Captain Trollope finally dropped anchor in the Downs, waiting for a fair wind, but was presently enveloped there by a clammy fog. A shore boat came alongside with eggs and butter and the bumboat woman was asked for news. 'General Grey has marched his sodgers into Chatham and Sheerness,' she called out, 'The mutineers aren't no longer allowed ashore!' The seamen heard and understood the implications of that. Then the fog thickened and there were no more shore boats. Captain Trollope fretted over the delay, irritably pacing the stern gallery. Grant found work for the men to do.

As for Delancey, who was on watch, he sensed some excitement among a few of the men. There was nothing tangible to report but he smelt trouble. A boat had been sent ashore soon after the ship anchored and was still alongside with a boatkeeper on board. Looking over the side, Delancey wondered idly why the boat was still in the water. Then he remembered that the plan had been to row guard, an order cancelled because of the fog. Uneasy about the situation, he went below to his cabin and picked up a brace of pistols, checked the priming and pushed them under the waistband of his breeches.

On deck again, he paced restlessly around. Looking over the ship's side he could see that the fog was as thick as ever. The sound of the pump working could be heard from a ship in the distance. A dog was barking on board another ship, nearer and in the opposite direction. Hearing a murmur of voices on the lower deck, he partly descended the fore hatch and paused there, looking forward and listening. A group of seamen, six or eight of them, were grouped round an object which he could not identify, a bundle of some sort. No regulation was being infringed and he returned to the quarterdeck, still very much on the alert.

Some minutes later he saw a group of men, probably the same group, approaching the forecastle. As the fog engulfed them he followed silently. When they reached the larboard cathead there was a violent dispute among the men. They surged to and fro, shouting and waving their arms. Suddenly there was a wild cry and next moment a body went spinning grotesquely over the side, hitting the water with a loud splash. There followed a loud cry of 'Man overboard!' repeated by half-a-dozen voices, and the whole group, now joined by others who were streaming from the forecastle, ran aft towards the larboard entry port.

Delancey was halfway up the starboard ladder leading to the forecastle when this happened. He scrambled down again, following the men aft and saw that several of them had pistols in their belts. They were obviously heading for the longboat, but they never reached it. Those in front came to a halt as Grant, appearing from nowhere, stood in front of them. There was a jostling and swearing among those behind, a recoil of those in front and the hubbub died away. In a moment of silence which followed there was a single pistol shot. Batley, who had been leading, swayed and then pitched forward on the deck with a dull thump. He lay moving convulsively, and Grant stood over him with a smoking pistol. A small pool of blood began to trickle towards the scuppers and one or two of the men made as if to pick Batley up.

'Leave him where he is,' was Grant's clear order, 'and stay where you are.' He was covering the men with his second pistol. 'You are all under arrest for mutiny and I'll shoot the first man who moves.' The marine posted as sentinel at the larboard entry port raised his musket at the same time, seeing which the other marine at the starboard entry did the same.

At this moment two or three of the seamen made as if to escape forward, thinking that they were unseen. Turning, they came face to face with Delancey, who was behind them with levelled pistols. 'Stay where you are,' he said. A boy came on deck from the fore-hatch and stared, open-mouthed, at the scene before him. 'Fetch the Master-at-Arms, boy,' called Delancey, 'and any of the marines you can find.' The boy fled and there was silence again, broken by Delancey who called out 'All those who are armed, drop your pistols on the deck.' It seemed for a moment as if the order would be disobeyed but the fall of one led to the fall of the others, four in number, one after the other. Batley rolled over with a pitiful groan, which Grant calmly ignored. From the rear of the group, just in front of Delancey, came Collins' voice:

'Look, Mr Grant, sir, there's a man overboard and we mean to rescue him. Can't leave him to drown, sir!'

Grant was about to reply when Captain Trollope appeared at his elbow, sword in hand.

'There is nobody overboard,' he said, 'only a dummy figure.' To the marine sentries he called out: 'Shoot any man who moves!' A whole minute passed in tense silence, broken only by

Batley's whimpering. 'Oh, God,' he groaned in a low voice, 'Oh, God—Oh, God,' Then the Master-at-Arms arrived on deck with two of his corporals and a dozen marines.

'Put these men in irons for attempted mutiny,' said Grant, his pistol still levelled. As the arrests were made he turned at last to Captain Trollope and said, very formally,

'I have to report, sir, that the mutiny on board the *Glatton* is over.'

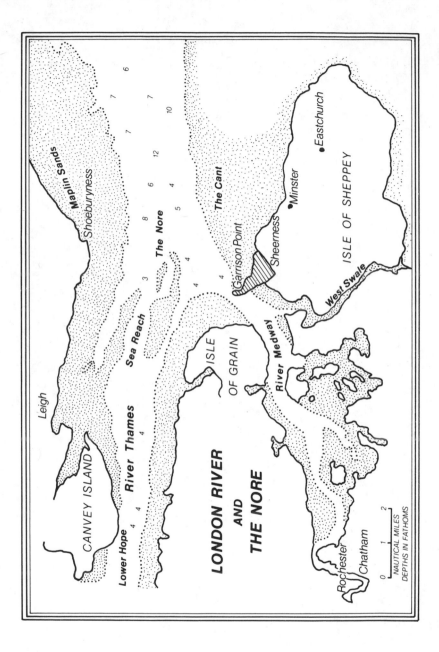

LONDON RIVER
AND
THE NORE

ISLE OF SHEPPEY

Eastchurch

Minster

Sheerness

Garrison Point

The Cant

West Swale

River Medway

ISLE
OF GRAIN

Rochester

Chatham

Maplin Sands

Shoeburyness

The Nore

Sea Reach

River Thames

Lower Hope

CANVEY ISLAND

Leigh

6
7
7
10
7
12
6
8   5   4
3   4   5
4   4
4
4
4   4

0   1   2
NAUTICAL MILES
DEPTHS IN FATHOMS

☆ ☆

CHAPTER THREE

The Court Martial

BATLEY did not die; at least, not immediately. The shot had missed his heart, lodging in his chest cavity on the right side where it was impossible to extract. The bullet had carried with it some fragments of clothing which caused gangrene. He lingered on for nearly a week and was even conscious for a day or two. During that space of time the fog lifted, the wind backed easterly and the *Glatton* entered the Thames Estuary, finally dropping anchor at the Nore. Batley was taken ashore to the naval hospital at Sheerness where he died on the following day. His adherents, sixteen in number, were lodged in the *Eagle* prison-hulk as prisoners awaiting court-martial. Captain Trollope had reported from the Downs on 5th June that he had subdued all disturbances on board the *Glatton,* now in a state of obedience. This was true enough and it was evident now that the mutiny at the Nore was drawing to a close. Several Lords of the Admiralty, headed by Lord Spencer himself, had come down to Sheerness, bringing with them a revised version of the royal pardon. They made it clear, however, that they would make no more concessions of any kind. Several ships now deserted the rebel fleet or 'floating republic', some going up river and others taking refuge under the shore batteries at Sheerness. The mutineers had lost heart, only a few ineffective shots being fired at the *Glatton* when she came into the fleet anchorage under her proper colours. One after another the red flags were hauled down and Richard Parker, leader of the mutineers, was arrested on June 14th. The mutiny had collapsed and the fact was reported to the Cabinet and to King George III. It remained to place the fleet in a state of discipline. It was going to take years.

Many seamen were tried in the following weeks and among them the men from the *Glatton*, accused of mutiny and attempted desertion. They lacked the man who had been their usual spokesman but Collins proved himself a good substitute. He argued on behalf of himself and his shipmates that their earlier misconduct was covered by the royal pardon and that the incident in the Downs did not amount to mutiny. They were acquitted on the main charge and convicted merely of attempted desertion. They were each sentenced to a year's hard labour and even this was remitted. Sent back to duty, they were dispersed among other ships, being lucky to escape a worse fate. But the verdict on the *Glatton*'s mutineers had an unforeseen result. If they had not been in a state of mutiny on the day of their arrest it could be argued that Batley was equally innocent on that charge. He had been killed, it would seem, while attempting to desert. There was thus a case against Grant for manslaughter, or even murder, and it fell to Captain Trollope to explain the situation to him.

'I cannot tell you how sorry I am,' he concluded, 'but Admiral Buckner feels that we have no alternative. You are to be court-martialled.'

'Do you think that is just, sir?'

'I cannot say that I do. But I want you to see it from his point of view. The leading mutineers at the Nore were dealt with severely, many of them hanged. Court members felt it their duty to make an example. Who shall blame them? The result, however, has been to create a revulsion among opposition members of Parliament. There have been critical comments in the newspapers and unpleasant questions in the House. The result was a certain leniency in the later trials and an evident desire to show that the proceedings have been fair. Senior officers are particularly anxious to show that justice has been impartial as between the seamen and their officers. To overlook your case might bring the navy into disrepute, it is thought, suggesting that lower deck men can be hanged for mere insolence whereas commissioned officers can do as they please.'

'So I am to be made the sacrifice . . .'

'You mustn't think so. I am confident that you will be acquitted.'

'I can be acquitted but still sacrificed. One of the captains put ashore by his crew has already shot himself.'

'Yes, I know that.'

'And who, sir, is to prosecute?'

'Technically speaking it has to be me. I shall call in another captain to assist me, however, more especially as I am also liable to be called as a witness.'

'But you must realise, sir, the danger to which I am exposed. A mutiny is more easily quelled at the outset. When a mutiny begins an officer, knowing this, shoots the ringleader. The mutiny is finished before it has fairly begun. Then the officer is accused of murder. He pleads in his defence that the mutiny was prevented by his action. Had it not been for his initiative the ship would have been seized by the mutineers and taken into an enemy port. But how is he to *prove* it? We can prove the seriousness of a riot only by letting it go on, with twenty killed instead of one. Suppress it instantly and you are left with no evidence that it ever took place.'

'Do I need telling that? But of this, too, I am sure: it is better for you to be tried and acquitted than to be the subject forever of innuendo and gossip.'

'Am I entitled to employ counsel?'

'Yes, you are. I doubt, however, whether it would be worth your while. You can call in a brother officer to assist you in your defence.'

'Thank you, sir, I'll do that. You think that my briefing counsel would prejudice the court against me?'

'Well, the prosecution being left to a layman, some members
of the court might wonder why the defence should not be left to
another. I have heard that view expressed.'

'I understand, sir, and will follow your advice.'

'Don't imagine that I like this business, Grant. I would to
God that it hadn't happened, and while I shall do my duty, I
hope that the prosecution will fail to prove its case. If you have
to be tried, moreover, I could wish that it were before a civilian
judge and jury. After the fright they have had in Chatham, and
after the damage done ashore by the mutineers, I doubt
whether they would think there was a case to answer. At Maidstone Assizes you would be acquitted without the defence being
even called. However, a court martial there has to be and I have
to tell you, with deep regret, that you are under open arrest.
This is a mere formality, of course, but I have no alternative.'

Following this unpleasant interview Grant went to visit
Delancey in his cabin. After repeating the gist of what the captain had said he went on rather hesitantly:

'I know that we are not especially close friends. We have not
always agreed on service matters and this I realise. But I have
come to respect your knowledge and judgment. Will you help
me in the conduct of my defence?'

Delancey was silent for a few moments and then replied: 'I
shall be happy to do my best. You will be wrong, however, if
you think me an expert in court procedure. I have never
attended a court martial save on the one occasion when I was a
witness, and that was done years ago.'

'I can think of no one better, for all that.'

'Very well then, I'll do my best. It so happens, moreover that
I have here on my shelf a book that may prove useful.' Delancey
found the volume and showed Grant the title page which read *A*

Treatise of the Principles and Practice of Naval Courts Martial, by John McArthur. Grant looked at the book in wonder.

'Who is John McArthur?' he asked.

'Former Judge-Advocate in North America, afterwards Secretary to Lord Hood. The book was published five years ago and cites precedents up to 1791. I shall now study them afresh. But I had better make a note, first, of the essential facts. Now tell me exactly what happened on June 5th. It was a Sunday, was it not?'

'Yes, the King's birthday by rights but that had to be observed the day before.'

'Just so. The ship was at anchor in the Downs. Had you any special reason to expect trouble?'

'Not more than on any other day since the mutiny began. I did have the feeling, however, that it was a case of now or never—for the ringleaders, I mean.'

'Because of the fog, you mean?'

'And because of the news from the Nore, that the mutiny there was likely to end.'

'So you were armed? . . .'

Covering sheet after sheet of paper, Delancey began to build up his case for the defence.

On board the *Glatton* there followed some days of preparation and growing tension. Under open arrest, Grant had meals in his cabin and appeared on deck at stated hours. The wardroom officers were careful never to refer to the coming trial but their avoidance of the topic made their conversation stilted and unreal. On the day before that chosen there were many boats coming and going, many hurried conferences and last minute instructions.

There was a still more tense atmosphere on the day itself (July 11th, 1797), heightened by the cleaning and polishing, by the rigging of the coloured side-ropes at the gangway, by the parading of the white-clad side boys and the careful inspection of the marine guard. There were many points of ceremony to be decided, as when it was asked whether the drums should beat a March. 'No, no!' said Pringle, '*Not* a March. That is reserved for an Admiral. For a Vice-Admiral the honours are laid down as follows: A Captain's Guard, a salute by all officers and three ruffles on the drum.'

Then the captains began to arrive, some from their ships in the anchorage, some in boats from the dockyard or from Sheerness. The side was piped for each and each was ceremoniously received at the main entry. The climax came with the approach of the Vice-Admiral's barge. The bugle sounded and the guard was called to attention, the bargemen tossed their oars as the boat came alongside. As Sir Thomas Pasley, Bart., came on deck the pipes twittered, the guard presented arms, the drums ruffled, swords were lowered and hands were raised in salute and a flag was broken out at the foremast. The court, it was clear, was about to assemble.

Apart from all the preparations on deck the great cabin had been transformed for the occasion. It was spacious, to begin with—the ship, after all, had been an East Indiaman—and a long table covered with green baize, rigged athwartships, took up nearly the whole width. There was a fine carved chair for the president with a velvet seat and gold tassels. This was on loan from the dockyard. The ten chairs flanking the presidential chair on either side were less ornate but still adequate. Ordinary wardroom chairs sufficed for others officially present but there was a leather-cushioned chair for the judge advocate. Some benches had been placed near the entrance for the public and it was known that two or three journalists would be present, one of them from London.

The doors were thrown open by a marine sergeant who was to act as usher and the members of the court strolled in with elaborate unconcern. The blue uniforms were brushed and speckless, the gold braid shone in the light from the stern-windows, the wigs were snowy white and the sword hilts glittered.

'Shall we be seated, gentlemen?' said Captain Sir Erasmus Gower after a glance at his watch. He himself set the example, taking the chair on the president's right while Captain Stanhope flanked the presidential chair on the other side. The other captains took their places with due regard for seniority and a shuffling noise came from outside the door where members of the public were waiting with some impatience.

A minute passed and then the doors were thrown open with a flourish and the marine sergeant announced the appearance of the Admiral President. All present rose to their feet and Sir Thomas strolled in, followed by the Judge Advocate, Mr Moses Greetham. Bows were exchanged and Sir Thomas took his seat, which was held for him by a young officer. The Judge Advocate went to the end of the table on the President's right, where his clerk had arranged some calf-bound volumes before him. The members of the court sat down again. At a nod from the President, Mr Pringle, sitting at the other end of the table, hurried to the door and gave an order to a midshipman. Within the minute a gun fired somewhere overhead and all present knew that a signal flag had broken out to indicate that the court martial had begun.

The Admiral President read out the Admiralty Order which constituted the court. Returning, Mr Pringle laid Grant's sword, lengthwise, on the table in front of the President. Then the doors were opened again and Grant came in, escorted by the Admiralty Marshal, Mr John Crickett, and stood facing the court behind a slight barrier. Members of the public were then allowed in, some with seats allocated and others having to stand at the back. Grant's identity being established, the charge was read by the Judge Advocate, who went on to state that both the prosecutor and the accused had asked to have the assistance of a brother officer in the presentation of the case. These officers were then recognised by the court.

So far, Delancey had been standing well back on the president's left and Captain Osborne, for the prosecution, had been as self-effacing on the president's right. Each now came forward and bowed to the court. Each was now provided, as if by magic, with a small table and chair. Looking across at Osborne, Delancey saw a short slim man with a sharp-looking and parchment coloured face, a senior captain and middle-aged. There was something vindictive about his look, as if he had come to the conclusion that Grant's conviction would be deserved and might even reflect some credit on the prosecution. Sweating slightly and feeling extremely nervous, Delancey was awed in the presence of so much seniority and daunted by the age and experience of his antagonist. He told himself sharply that he had a duty to perform, that the trial had begun and that he would need his wits about him.

The trial proceeded on its ponderous course, basic facts being established by routine questions. As regards the general situation on board the *Glatton* previous to June 5th there was indeed a measure of agreement among the witnesses. There had been mutiny on board the ship, revealed not by acts of violence but merely by a refusal to obey certain orders, as also by the crew's insistence that the ship should go to Spithead instead of remaining with Admiral Duncan's flag. After the ship reached Spithead the crew had behaved well but had still refused to give up the arms they had improperly seized. They were still, therefore, technically in a state of mutiny when the ship dropped anchor in the Downs. She was then on passage to the Nore but was prevented by contrary winds and later by fog from entering the Thames Estuary. These facts were not in dispute. The court was at pains to establish the exact density of the fog, the limitation on visibility and the relative calm which prevailed at the time. At what distance from the shore was the

Glatton anchored? Could other ships be seen? On all these points the witnesses were pretty well agreed. Then Captain Trollope was called for the prosecution, being examined by Captain Osborne. The atmosphere, hitherto relaxed, became suddenly tense.

'Will you tell the Court, Captain, why you were on passage to the Nore?'

'I acted under orders from the Port Admiral at Portsmouth.'

'And were these orders explained to you?'

'Yes, sir. In the first place the *Glatton* came under Admiral Duncan's command and, but for the mutiny, would have been with his flag. It was my duty in fact to rejoin him as soon as I was in a position to do so.'

'But that, surely, would have implied sailing for Yarmouth or for the Texel?'

'Yes, sir. My crew, however, had a grievance in that they had not been paid for fifteen months. They could be paid only at Chatham, where the ship was commissioned. By going to the Nore, on the way to Yarmouth, I was agreeing, in effect, with one of the crew's more reasonable demands.'

'Thank you, sir. Would you agree then that a further mutiny, with a violence not hitherto known, would be most unlikely while the ship was on her passage to the Nore?'

Delancey was on his feet in an instant.

'Admiral President, sir, I must protest against a question designed to entrap the witness into an expression of opinion.'

After a short whispered discussion with the more senior captains the President allowed the question, but the intervention had given Trollope the necessary warning. After the question had been repeated he replied very deliberately:

'The crew wanted their pay but ringleaders in the mutiny had reason to fear that they might be singled out for punishment, as had happened indeed to many others. Some of them might be thought to have had a motive for violence.'

Captain Osborne looked annoyed but went on to the next question:

'Will you describe to the court, Captain, the events of June 5th in so far as you observed them?'

'Halfway through the first dog-watch—'

'Can you be more precise, sir?'

'At a few minutes after five o'clock I heard what seemed to be a disturbance on deck. There was some confused shouting which ended with the sound of a shot. I sent my servant with an order to the marines to parade at once, fully armed. I fetched my sword and, in doing so, chanced to look out of the larboard port, I think to see whether the fog was still thick. I saw, floating alongside, drifting aft, a dummy figure in wood and canvas. I then came on to the quarterdeck, followed by the marine who had been at my cabin door. I saw a group of seamen confronted by Mr Grant, pistol in hand. One man was lying, wounded, on the deck.'

'What happened after that?'

'One of the seamen called out that there was a man overboard and that he should be saved. I replied that no one had gone overboard, only a dummy figure. I told the marines— there were three, including the one at my heels—to shoot any man who moved. A minute or two later the Master-at-Arms arrived and the men under arrest were taken below.'

'Did Mr Grant say anything to you?'

'Yes, sir, he did. He reported to me that the mutiny in the *Glatton* was over.'

'Did he refer to the mutiny of the past weeks or did you take it that he referred to the events of that day?'

Delancey was on his feet again:

'I submit, sir, that this question is improper in form. The witness has no means of knowing what the accused meant.' When the objection was upheld Osborne looked flustered and upset. He went on, however:

'One final question. We have heard from another witness that the wounded seaman (or, rather, landsman), Thomas Batley, was then carried to the sickbay. Was this done on your orders or on orders from Mr Grant?'

'On my orders, sir.'

'Thank you, captain.'

Captain Trollope was then cross-examined by Delancey.

'When Mr Grant spoke to you, immediately after you came on deck, did you make any reply?'

'Yes, I did. I said "Well done!" I thought then and believe now that he acted very properly.'

'Will you tell the court, sir, what you think of Mr Grant as an officer?'

'He is, I think, one of the best first lieutenants I have ever known. He is a good seaman, a fine disciplinarian, a man whose courage has been proved in battle, a man generally liked by his messmates, an officer much admired by the crew.'

'Thank you, sir. No further questions.'

Other witnesses followed, the surgeon, the master-at-arms, a marine sergeant, a volunteer (2nd class), the boatswain and the boatkeeper. The story of what happened was by now well established and with little conflict of evidence. The case for the prosecution was closed and Delancey called on Grant to give evidence.

He told the court at the same time that he was calling no other witness for the defence. Grant moved to the witness stand and took the oath before facing the court.

'You are first lieutenant, are you not, of His Majesty's Ship *Glatton*?'

'Yes, sir.'

'For how long have you served in that capacity?'

'Since she was commissioned in 1795.'

'Have you anything to add to the evidence the Court has already heard about events previous to June 5th?'

'No, sir.'

'Will you tell the Court, in your own words, what your part was in the events of that day?'

'The *Glatton* was at anchor in the Downs on passage from Spithead to the Nore. A contrary wind had prevented our sailing and then there was fog. With the mutiny ended at Spithead, with news that the mutiny was likely to end at the Nore, I felt that the ringleaders among our own crew might resort to violence when they began to lose their former sense of power. I was especially watchful, therefore, knowing also that the fog would discourage or prevent the intervention of loyal ships.'

'You went armed for that reason?'

'All officers were armed at that time.'

'No doubt.' Delancey was gaining confidence.

'Will you now tell the Court, sir, how you first came to realise that trouble of some sort was impending?'

'I find it difficult to explain. There were unusual movements and whisperings, men looking furtive and trying to be casual. A first lieutenant learns to sense trouble, I think. During the first dog watch there was an outcry. I have been told since that it was a call of 'Man overboard!' To me it seemed no more at the time than a confused noise. I was on the quarterdeck but ran towards the larboard entry port.'

'May I ask why, sir?'

'Because the longboat was there, already in the water. An emergency in harbour often requires the use of a boat.'

'Just so. And then?' Delancey carefully avoided giving Grant a lead.

'I heard and saw a crowd of seamen running aft from the direction of the forecastle. A number of them were armed and foremost among them were men I recognised as ringleaders in the mutiny. I drew the two pistols I had tucked into my waistband. On seeing me the men hesitated for an instant. Aiming carefully, I fired at the man who was foremost, who fell to the deck. I put the remainder under arrest for attempted mutiny.'

'And the man wounded was Thomas Batley?'

'Yes, sir.'

'And what, did you suppose, was the object of the men he led?'

'I had no doubt that their intention was to seize the ship, killing or confining the officers.'

'Was the wind fair for Holland, had they wished to take the ship into an enemy port?'

'Yes, sir. It was a nor'westerly wind.'

'You have learnt since that the mutineers—'

It was Captain Osborne's turn to interrupt:

'I protest, sir, against Mr Delancey assuming what he has to prove. I should be less at fault if I referred to them as "deserters."'

'I submit, sir,' said Delancey, slightly nettled, 'that most of the seamen, including those to whom I refer, were and had been for days in a state of mutiny.'

'That I accept,' said the Admiral. 'It will save disagreement, however, if you will describe this group of men as the malcontents.'

'I am happy to accept that term, sir,' said Delancey with a bow. 'May I continue?' The Admiral nodded.

'You have learnt since, Mr Grant, that the malcontents had designs on the longboat. We all realise that you did not know this at the time. Do you now agree that their aim was to desert rather than mutiny?'

'No, sir. What they did or intended was consistent with attempting to capture another and perhaps smaller vessel anchored in the vicinity. Except for that purpose their pistols would have been needless. Such a capture as they may have intended would have been a further act of mutiny, perhaps indeed of piracy.'

'We have no evidence, have we, of any such plan?'

'No, sir. The prevention of the deed deprives us of knowing exactly what was intended.'

'Thank you, Mr Grant. No more questions.'

Captain Osborne now cross-examined the witness.

'Would I be right in concluding, Mr Grant, that you regarded Batley as the guiding spirit of the mutiny?'

'He was the principal spokesman for the mutineers and may well have been the actual leader.'

'*Was* he, in your opinion, the leader?'

'I have no means of knowing.'

'But you thought him a dangerous man?'

'Yes.'

'You thought that the ship, without him, would soon return to naval discipline?'

'The *Glatton* is now in a state of discipline.'

'No doubt. But was that your belief on June 5th? That this one man's death would end the mutiny?'

Delancey intervened quickly:

'I protest, sir, against a line of questioning designed to entrap the accused. He has told the court why he fired when he did. He fired to prevent the immediate violence which he had every reason to apprehend.'

There was a minute's pause at the end of which the Admiral said slowly: 'I allow the question. The accused must answer.' The question was now repeated and Grant replied:

'I did not shoot this man as a bad character. I shot him as the foremost man in a crowd which was apparently intent on violence.'

'You did not single him out as generally dangerous?'

'No, sir.'

'Did it occur to you that these men were merely trying to desert the ship?'

'I must accept this as the verdict of another court martial. I had no idea of it at the time.'

'But you knew that the longboat was alongside?'

'Yes, sir. It would still have been my duty to prevent desertion even had I known that these men were potential deserters rather than mutineers.'

'But was it your duty to arrest, question, investigate, prosecute, try, condemn and execute this man, all in the time it took you to press the trigger?'

Delancey was on his feet but the Admiral was even quicker, saying:

'The accused need not answer that question.'

On re-examination by Delancey, Grant was asked:

'Had you wished to get rid of this man as a bad influence, would you not agree that his desertion would have served your purpose as well as his death has done?'

'Yes, sir,' said Grant. 'I repeat, however, that I fired at the man who was foremost in the riot. That he was also a bad influence generally was a coincidence.'

That concluded the evidence given by the accused and the Admiral, looking at his watch, decided that the court had sat for long enough. He rose to his feet and said:

'This would seem a convenient moment to end our proceedings for the day. The Court stands adjourned and will reconvene in the same place at nine o'clock tomorrow morning.' The other members of the Court all rose at this, bowed to the President and began to disperse. There was a general buzz of conversation and the reporters were seen hurrying for the shore. Several captains went back to their own ships, others had agreed to dine with each other and three of them were to dine with the Commissioner of the Dockyard. On board the *Glatton* again, Delancey had a talk with Grant, telling him that he had given his evidence very well. Privately, he was worried by the situation and all too dubious about the probable result.

The next day was cloudless and the *Glatton* was the scene of the same ritual again. One effect of a court martial was to make an exhibit of the ship in which the trial was being held. While the proceedings lasted she would be under the critical eye of flag officers, rival captains, censorious first lieutenants and even some members of the public. The quest for perfection extended even to each boat that swept alongside. The dress of the seamen generally was not uniform—it had merely to be clean, tidy and seamanlike—but boats' crews were clad uniformly at each captain's expense. Each boat was smartly painted with a touch of gold leaf at the bow and stern, each crew had its own style and all the oarsmen were trained to toss their oars upright as the boat surged up to the entry port. Watching this performance with admiration, Delancey hoped that there was justification in the belief that men who were smart on parade would be good in battle. Judged by that standard everyone in sight should be a tiger in action. But was it true? Half the seamen visible had been quite recently in a state of mutiny. Some had been lucky to escape a noose at the yardarm. They might look impressive now on a sunny morning but the fact remained that gleaming brasswork had been consistent with disloyalty. He put the thought from him and went to take his place in the great cabin where the court was very nearly assembled. The side was piped once more as he did so, marking the arrival of the last captain. Ten minutes later the Admiral President took his seat and the court was called to order.

'During yesterday's proceedings, gentlemen,' said the presiding Admiral, 'we heard all the witnesses listed, concluding with the evidence of the accused, called as witness for the defence. I now call upon the prosecuting officer to summarise the case for the prosecution.'

As Captain Osborne rose to address the court, Delancey glanced along the row of captains and tried to guess what their verdict would be. These were practically the same men who had so recently condemned Richard Parker to death. Now was their chance to show their impartiality. Mutineers were not to be shot by outraged first lieutenants. They must be brought to trial in the proper way, sentenced with the proper words and hanged with all due solemnity and the yellow flag hoisted over all. Watching their faces, Delancey thought that Grant's case had been tried beforehand and was already lost. Osborne, meanwhile, was making a clear summary of the evidence, going through the story of the mutiny and describing how Batley came to be shot. He did not make the mistake of blackening Grant's character. He was at pains rather to show that it takes a good man to commit a certain kind of crime. He was as far again from making the opposite mistake by representing Batley as a martyr for some noble cause. He was careful (curse him!) over his facts, his times and dates, leaving Delancey without an excuse to interrupt.

Listening to the skilled and persuasive monologue, Delancey found himself absently fingering his copy of McArthur, flipping the pages at random. Suddenly his attitude changed and he read more carefully. . . . Then he read it again. Could that be right? Was that the answer? He marked two places with slips of paper and sat back with a frown. If he was right, how did it come about that no one else had seen it? How could the judge advocate have overlooked so obvious a point? With an effort he brought himself back to the immediate present and to the sound of Osborne's pitiless summary:

'I am not urging the court to think of Batley as a loyal subject, a fine seaman, a loss to the service. He was none of these things. Had he lived much longer he might well have had to face a capital charge. Over the years since the *Glatton* was commissioned he had been a bad influence among the crew. On this subject you have heard the evidence of the Master-at-Arms. Batley, it is clear, was at once useless and covertly insolent, doing all he could to undermine discipline while remaining just within the letter of the law. It could never be said of him that he had struck a superior officer or disobeyed a direct order. He had not stolen nor had he been found drunk. It was his role rather to encourage others in misconduct while he himself remained in the background. I do not ask the Court to shed any tears over this man. I would merely suggest that every other ship has just such a character and that each one is detested by the junior officers. The *Glatton*'s cunning rebel was no exception in this. There came the moment, however, when he had at last to show his hand. He made himself prominent during a time of open mutiny. As the movement died away, all reasonable demands being met by our gracious sovereign, Batley saw that his hour of authority was coming to an end. With the ship at anchor in a fog, with the longboat alongside, with the shore not far distant, he and his accomplices resolved to desert. It was Batley's notion to accomplish this design by raising the cry 'Man overboard!' so that the rush for the longboat would seem to be natural and justified. But when the moment came to seize the boat these deluded men found themselves face-to-face with the tireless, vigilant and fearless first lieutenant. Did they rush at him, waving such weapons as they had? Did they call for help from their shipmates? Did they brazen it out, repeating their false cry of 'Man overboard'? They did nothing of the kind. They wavered, shame-faced, like children discovered in an orchard, like thieves caught in the act. They had no idea what to do or which way to look. Their little plot was discovered and they faced the painful consequences.

'Look at the situation now from the point of view of the accused. We have heard evidence which shows him to be an admirable officer in every way, and this evidence I, for one, am glad to accept. He is proud of his ship which has recently fought an action which we shall none of us forget. He is also proud of her active officers and promising midshipmen, of her well-trained and disciplined crew. He looks again with pride on her white decks, her bright paintwork, her neatly flaked ropes, her gleaming steel, her polished brass. Looking about us, we all realise, surely, that we are aboard a smart ship. Now imagine what it must feel like to have this ship and crew marred by a small group of mutineers, a centre of sedition, a source of infection from which the poison spreads outward to corrupt the whole? To a good lieutenant, to such a man as the accused, the mere existence of this dissident group was a daily affront—something like some pitch spilt on an otherwise spotless quarterdeck. Leader of the group was this man Batley. Came the moment, on June 5th, when there was a scene of open disorder. Perhaps as many as twenty men made an attempt to desert. It might have seemed like a mutiny, a planned attempt to capture the ship. We know now that it was not, that the men involved were too few to have done this, but I for one would concede that this riot might have had the appearance of a violent mutiny. As against that, the violence died away as soon as the lieutenant appeared. And while these foolish men hesitated, a mere word being enough to quell them, the accused officer, Mr Grant, levelled his pistol and pressed the trigger. The leader of this dissident gang, Batley himself, lay dying at the feet of the accused.

'It is no easy task for me to prosecute so good an officer as the accused. Could it be that Batley was victimised? Did Mr Grant yield to this temptation? I do not profess to know. Let us suppose, however, that there was no malice in Mr Grant, only a deep concern for his ship. Here was a centre of infection to be rooted out and he did what seemed necessary. Many of us here might have wished to do the same and we should all agree, perhaps, that Batley was no loss to the service. The fact remains, however, and this is the central fact in my case, that the misconduct of which Batley was guilty is not a capital offence. And even if it were, that capital sentence would have to be passed by a court martial, not by a single officer. But Batley was also guilty, I shall be reminded, of attempted desertion. So he was. And had he been caught in the act of desertion—had he been in the boat and pulling away—a shot fired at him would have been justified even had it proved fatal. It would have been fired in order to prevent desertion. But that was not the actual situation. The attempt to desert the ship had been abandoned. The men were at a stand, looking foolish; and it was at that instant that the shot was fired. However much sympathy we may have for the accused—and I have myself the deepest sympathy—we cannot allow it to be thought that we allow discipline to be enforced in this way. It is my painful duty to ask the Court for a verdict of guilty.'

Captain Osborne sat down and Delancey knew that the case was lost as far as that court was concerned. Osborne had put the case for the prosecution extremely well, taking care to praise Grant as an officer and basing his final address on a point of law. There was no real defence, although a more sympathetic court might well, and probably would, produce a different verdict. He had only one card to play and he could not be certain that it was a trump. Making a quick decision he rose to his feet with assumed confidence when called upon to make his final address:

'Admiral President, sir, it is with real concern that I have to raise at this time a point of law which should more properly have been discussed at the beginning of the trial. It is my duty to ask, on behalf of the accused, whether this court has the power to try this case at all.'

There was a sudden change of atmosphere, an almost audible gasp, and the presiding admiral looked sternly at Delancey as if he had uttered blasphemy in open court. The Judge Advocate was even more shocked and the more senior captains went red in the face. Sir Thomas Pasley spoke very gravely:

'I hope that Lieutenant Delancey realises the seriousness of what he has just suggested. I hope he is not about to waste the time of the court on a frivolous plea. I deem it my duty, nevertheless, to hear what his plea is. You may continue, Mr Delancey, but I hope you will be brief.'

'Thank you, sir. We have had evidence to show that Tom Batley was wounded by a pistol fired on board this ship. We have also had evidence to show that he actually died while ashore at Sheerness. Had he died while at sea Mr Grant would have been liable to be tried by court martial. He died, however, on land, which brings his death within the jurisdiction of the civil courts. The precedents are clear. When Richard Davis killed John Liddel Palmer aboard the *Eurydice* in 1783, Davis was court-martialled because the deceased had died at sea. But when Lieutenant Osmond stabbed Richard Tucker in 1782, the wounded man subsequently dying in Haslar Hospital, the trial took place in the county where he died. The question of jurisdiction in such cases is covered, I submit, by statute, 2 Geo. II C. 21. "When a person shall be feloneously stricken upon the sea and shall die of the stroke in England, the offender must be indicted in the county where the death shall happen."'

There was a shocked silence, broken finally by the presiding admiral:

'May I ask, Mr Delancey, why you said nothing of this when the trial began?'

'Because, sir, the point has only recently been brought to my attention. I am not a lawyer by profession.'

At this the Judge Advocate, who *was* a lawyer by profession, went to confer with the Admiral President, who presently announced that the court would adjourn, resuming its session in one hour's time. When the court sat again the presiding admiral made a brief and final announcement:

'In accordance with statute 2 Geo. II C. 21 this case will be referred to the civil authorities in the County of Kent. This court is now dissolved.'

There was a buzz of conversation and some unfriendly looks directed towards the defending officer. Captain Trollope came over, however, and shook Delancey by the hand. 'You have certainly made your reputation as a lawyer! Well done, indeed!'

Grant was quite touchingly grateful. 'You turned the tables on Osborne at the eleventh hour! What an astonishing performance! And there is no doubt, I am told, about the verdict ashore.' Even Sir Thomas Pasley had a kind word for him. 'Well, Mr Delancey, your friend was lucky to have you as his advocate. Some senior officers may think you too clever by half, but I won't accept that. We should have known the law better than we did. I shall hope to hear some day, however, that you have used as much tactical skill against the enemy.'

Trollope answered for Delancey's prowess in action and ended by saying: 'We have spent time enough in fighting each other. It is time we began fighting the Dutch!'

✩ ✩

CHAPTER FOUR

The Tempest

ONE BY ONE, Admiral Duncan's ships returned to him. Because of the court-martial the *Glatton* was one of the last to appear with Richard Delancey as acting first lieutenant, a temporary replacement for Alexander Grant. Captain Trollope felt, and with some reason, that he was himself responsible for Grant's predicament. It was his duty, he believed, to see Grant reinstated in the service. The result of the trial had also increased his respect for Delancey, whom he thought a perfectly acceptable substitute for Grant. If there was anyone dubious about this substitution it was Delancey himself, who would rather have gained experience in a smaller and more typical ship. What he wanted was the command of a sloop with someone like Grant as first lieutenant. In Delancey's opinion, Grant was the ideal first lieutenant for the brilliant but sometimes erratic Trollope and he never supposed that he himself would be half as good.

As the *Glatton* came in sight of Admiral Duncan's flag, Delancey thought over the duties which went with his new, if acting, position. He had one or two privileges, as in standing no watch and in having the aftermost cabin on the starboard side. Inside his cabin hung the keys of the magazines in a place known only to the other lieutenants, and never delivered to anyone but the gunner. Outside his cabin hung the keys of the store rooms. These might be said to symbolise his wide responsibilities and his load of detailed and varied work. It was he who drew up the watch, station and quarter bills— the assignment of every man on board to his place for purposes of work, battle and sleep. It was his responsibility to ensure that each watch, each gun-crew, was balanced as between experience and relative ignorance, as between youth and age. He had to watch the men at work or in action, making a mental note of all who might deserve promotion. He had to have an eagle eye for the slightest defect, whether a frayed rope or some blistered paintwork. He had to believe what Grant used to repeat, that there is no excuse for anything. On the quarterdeck he was to be the very embodiment of naval discipline, exacting, precise, clear and brief. In emergency he must be a tower of strength, confident, cheerful and brave. With more than enough courage and presence of mind for his own needs, he must be able to share these qualities with everyone else, distributing confidence from an apparently inexhaustible supply. He had to be everywhere, with the right word for each man aboard, encouragement for one and reproof for another. On occasion he might laugh when expected to reprimand. On rare occasions he should fail to notice, looking the other way. But his task, in general, was to maintain a finely-adjusted fighting machine, all material resources so arranged as to be found in an instant, all human resources employed to the best advantage throughout the day and night.

Performing all these duties, Delancey had also to change his role in a flash. From the moment Trollope appeared on deck he had to move aside and assume his position as a loyal subordinate. From the moment he entered the wardroom Delancey was merely the first among equals, ready even to share in a joke at his own expense. But even this measure of equality was not unqualified for it was also his duty to intervene as mediator should there be the least sign of friction. He might similarly have to mediate between the warrant officers—the master, the gunner, the boatswain, the sailmaker—each of them an important man, head of his own department. He had likewise to keep an eye on the young gentlemen, watching their progress in navigation and seamanship, being quick to intervene if any one of them seemed to be bullying the others. All these and a hundred other duties would have fallen to any first lieutenant but the *Glatton* brought with her some additional problems of her own. She had not been designed as a man-of-war, least of all as one with her peculiar armament. She was undermanned for her artillery and yet with crowded mess-decks. Delancey himself was to be regarded as a stopgap, a substitute for Mr Grant who would eventually reappear. Each routine and drill was of Grant's devising and there would have been resistance to any change. Delancey's position was far from enviable in more ways than one. He wondered from the beginning whether his best was good enough.

Delancey had also to remember that the *Glatton* formed part of a fleet in close formation and in presence of the enemy. His first duty, more immediate than any duty so far listed, was to keep station and watch the flagship for signals. With the Dutch fleet apparently ready to sail, Admiral Duncan kept his own force in tight formation on a given bearing and at a stated interval. Any blunder made by one ship would have been seen by all the rest and marked by a caustic signal from the flagship. The *Glatton* took her place in the line but was on a lower establishment with fewer officers and midshipmen. The lookout for signals was maintained with more difficulty, a midshipman in each watch having no other duty. A minor responsibility of the signals officer was to have a Bible at hand in case the signal should consist of book, chapter and verse. Duncan was too religious a man to misuse holy writ in this way but the fleet sometimes sailed as two squadrons and Vice-Admiral Onslow had no such inhibitions and was gifted with a sense of humour. Credit was gained by the ship which replied most quickly and appropriately in the same idiom. Delancey worried over this but worried still more to think that the whole fleet was in shallow water among sandbanks on the Dutch coast and potentially on a lee shore. There was hazard enough for any ship but the queerly armed *Glatton* was doubly at risk and had often been described as a floating coffin. With all the respect he had for Captain Trollope, and indeed for the absent Mr Grant, Delancey would not be sorry to see the last of the *Glatton*.

So far as loyalty went, the *Glatton*'s crew were above average. As against that, nobody could suppose that the results of the mutiny could be removed and forgotten in weeks or even in months. That there were malcontents on board was soon apparent. Delancey became gradually aware of them as the weeks of blockade duty went by. Trouble centred on two messes and on two contrasting characters, one the purser's steward and the other the caulker's mate. The first of these, Thomas Bascomb, a former baker's man, was literate and talkative and had been one of the 'delegates' on board the *Repulse*. His early submission had saved him from court martial but he remembered his brief moment of power and hoped that revolution in some form might still be possible. Left to himself he was too weak to do more than mutter veiled threats in a corner. Under the influence of loyal messmates he might have become a useful member of the crew. He had fallen, instead, under the influence of Jacob Fuller, a more sinister character whose background was that of a seaman in a Liverpool slaver. Fuller had been in the *Glatton* during the mutiny but had played no part in the movement which the officers had finally suppressed. This was not, apparently, because he was loyal to the captain but because he had been on bad terms with Batley and Donovan. He appeared to have an undue influence over his messmates, who were evidently afraid of him. His manner was surly, especially to the petty officers, but he had not so far committed any offence. The master-at-arms looked on these two groups with suspicion but had gone no further than warning them against being insolent. There was no reason to believe that his warning had produced any lasting effect.

In dealing with potential sedition there are several rules, as Delancey well knew; one being to give the men something else to think about, another being to be ruthless at the outset. The longer action is delayed the more bloody it has to be. While meaning to be fair, Delancey was not averse to making an example of Fuller or Bascomb if either of them were to step out of line. As luck would have it, they both did, being guilty of insolence towards the boatswain. Neither had disobeyed an order or struck a superior officer. They had used abusive language, however, and they had promptly been put in irons. The case was reported to the captain who allowed a day to elapse before hearing the evidence. There was little doubt about the facts, the boatswain's statement being corroborated by a ship's corporal, but Captain Trollope consulted Delancey before awarding sentence.

'The two men are different in character, sir,' replied Delancey, 'Fuller is the leader, Bascomb a weaker man led astray by bad example. I suggest that Fuller should be punished and Bascomb given a fright.'

'The difficulty about that is that each has committed the same offence.'

'Very true, sir. I think it possible, however, that Bascomb's messmates might stand surety for him.'

'Very well. Give a hint to the boatswain, who can have a word with them. In the meanwhile—a dozen each.'

In the matter of the punishment list ships varied enormously. There were ships in which discipline was severe, others (like the *Grampus*) in which flogging was almost unknown. There were few officers (and fewer lower deck men) who thought that it could be abolished entirely. During the height of the mutiny the seamen's demands had never included the abolition of the cat-

and-nine-tails. They had put some martinets ashore but they had themselves used the cat on one or two unpopular midshipmen, having no idea that it could be thought needless. Far from that, they all knew that life was worse under an easygoing captain, for the idle men could then escape notice, allowing the work to fall unevenly on those who were willing. Quite apart from this there was the question of the ship's safety. If the look-out-men dozed off, if the helmsman was thinking of something else, if someone smoked tobacco in the cable tier or painter's store, if a lantern were taken into the magazine, every man on board could lose his life. Older seamen realised this and were emphatic on the need for discipline in its most severe form. How else would the youngsters be taught to think of the ship first, of themselves afterwards?

The *Glatton* was a ship in which the cat was seldom used, Captain Trollope being at once humane and clever, well able to devise other punishments. It was never applied as a punishment for ignorance or unintentional blunder, being reserved for those who deliberately flouted authority. There was perhaps one flogging a month on an average, usually of a dozen strokes or less. Delancey knew that Captain Trollope was just and humane. He himself knew that flogging was necessary. What he hated was the actual sight and sound. He had been present at floggings enough—almost daily in the *Artemis*—but there was now a new element in the situation. He had previously been no more than a reluctant witness or the officer, on occasion, whose authority the captain was supporting. As first lieutenant, he was now the man all but directly responsible. More than that, the captain's absence would leave him in command so that the actual sentence would be his. For a sensitive man this was a burden which no sense of usage or habit could entirely remove.

Next day, August 30th, was sunny with a steady breeze and the fleet was close-hauled in two columns. In another hour the ships would wear together and resume their sentry-go in the opposite direction. Inshore, close to the Texel, were the two frigates whose task was to watch the enemy. Halfway between them and Duncan's flagship was a cutter, moving with the fleet, which repeated signals from and to the frigates. The rear ship of Onslow's column, the *Glatton* was exactly in station, her sails precisely trimmed, her decks white, the blue ensign fluttering at her mizzen peak. Delancey, pausing for a moment in his round of the decks, stood looking at the other column, ten ships in exact order with the *Venerable*, Duncan's flagship, in the centre of the line. The sea was green, swept with cloud shadows, the sunlight caught the sails and each ship's stem was hidden by foam. Delancey knew no sight more lovely combining as it did the beauty of nature with the order created by man. He had seen it a hundred times but it never failed to thrill him. Looking across at that precisely ordered line, he reflected for a minute on the invention and thought, on the discipline and work which made that tight formation possible. Some two hundred years of effort had gone to the forming of such a fleet; beautiful, ordered, menacing. . . .

His reverie was interrupted by a midshipman who touched his hat and said, 'Beg pardon, sir—it's within ten minutes of six bells.' Delancey looked round with a smile, saying, 'Thank you, Doyle. Pass the word to the Master-at-Arms and boatswain's mates.' He went to his cabin, where his servant handed him his sword and brushed a few specks off his uniform coat. A few minutes later he was in the half-deck and at the door of the captain's fore cabin or office. He knocked and entered, his cocked hat under his left arm, and stood at attention.

'Nearly six bells, sir.'

'Thank you, Delancey. Only two names in the list, I see.'

'Yes, sir.'

Captain Trollope took his sword off a hook, picked up the list and was handed his hat. As Delancey opened the door and stood aside, the captain went on deck, where the officer of the watch reported to him. As six bells were made (11.0 a.m.) the captain said, 'Turn the hands aft to witness punishment.' A midshipman scurried off and the order was piped and shouted. The marines fell in, dressed by the right and fixed bayonets. The other lieutenants, supported by the midshipmen, took post behind the captain on the weather side of the quarter-deck; the surgeon and purser on the lee side, with the boatswain and his mates in front of them. The ship's company collected in the area forward of the main-mast but in no particular order.

'Rig the gratings,' was the next order and the carpenter and his mates dragged two gratings aft, placing one on the deck and lashing the other upright against the ship's side.

'Jacob Fuller,' called the captain, and Fuller was brought forward by the master-at-arms.

'Jacob Fuller,' said the captain, loudly enough for all to hear. 'You have been guilty of negligence and of using abusive language to a superior officer, namely the boatswain. You have infringed the Articles of War, knowing what the penalty would be. Have you anything to say?' Fuller still looked defiant and surly but said nothing. The next order was brief:

'Strip.' Fuller took off his shirt and walked forward to the gratings where he stood on the one and extended his arms against the other.

'Seize him up,' said the captain and two quartermasters appeared with lengths of spun-yarn with which they secured Fuller's wrists to the grating. A piece of leather was given him to bite on, so as to prevent him biting his tongue.

'Seized up, sir,' they reported.

Captain Trollope now produced a copy of *The Articles of War*, removed his hat (all others present doing the same) and started reading out: 'Article Nineteen. If any Person in or belonging to the Fleet shall make or endeavour to make any mutinous Assembly upon any Pretence whatsoever . . .'

While the Articles were being read out, the senior boat-swain's mate opened a red baize bag, producing from it the red-handled cat—a wooden handled instrument with nine two-foot lengths of cord attached. Delancey thought grimly how few landsmen knew the real meaning of the expression 'letting the cat out of the bag'—the cat having nine lives or lashes. When the reading finished the captain gave the order:

'Do your duty.'

The boatswain's mate took position on Fuller's left, facing inboard, drew back the cat to its full length, separating the tails with his fingers, and laid on the first stroke. The noise it made was a dull thud, the blow being delivered by an extremely powerful arm. It left a dark weal across Fuller's bare shoulders. The cat was flung back again and fell once more, a fraction lower and making another dark line. The third stroke fell on the man's writhing body where the first had done, the dark weal turning to red; the fourth was a repetition of the second, with the skin cut open again; the fifth came lower and the sixth on nearly the same place. At this point the cat was handed to another boatswain's mate, who separated the nine tails (now stuck together with blood) and laid on the seventh stroke below the mark left by the sixth. . . . The last of all fell just above Fuller's waist, leaving his whole back more or less cut to rib-bons and bleeding. At last it was over and Fuller was cut down, given his shirt and taken below to the sick-bay for treatment. Once more discipline had been upheld and Delancey told him-self that there was no other way.

Watching this flogging, as he had watched so many others, and feeling slightly sick (as he always did) Delancey wondered what it felt like to the victim. He had been punished with a rope's end or starter as a boy. He had felt the cane as a midship-man. He had served with officers who had risen from the lower deck and one of them had described for him the agony of it. 'The first stroke,' he had said, 'drives the breath out of you.

After that each successive stroke is worse.' He had gone on to say that the hours of waiting, the time spent on preliminaries, added up to a different sort of hell.

Thinking of this, Delancey watched the face of Bascomb, whose turn was to follow. He was deadly pale, his features working as he realised the horror of it all, and only a ship's corporal's grasp prevented him from falling. Each thud of the falling lash made him wince as if he himself had been hit. And each thud, as he knew, brought the time nearer when his own punishment would begin. His lips were moving as if in prayer for a miracle that would save him. Trembling violently, he stared with a horrible fascination at Fuller's bleeding back, at the blood that was trickling to the deck. The dozen lashes took about fifty seconds to inflict, an eternity to the victim and as endless a period for the man who was to suffer next. Now Bascomb's name was called out. He was propelled forward by the master-at-arms and stood, shivering, before Captain Trollope.

'Thomas Bascomb,' said the captain. 'You have been found guilty of negligence and of using abusive language to a superior officer, namely the boatswain of this ship. You have infringed the Articles of War, knowing what the penalty would be. Have you anything to say?'

Bascomb broke into an incoherent flood of excuse and protest:

'Please, sir, I was led astray, following a bad example—never meant to offend—meant nothing by what I said—have humbly apologised to the boatswain—never meant no harm—won't never again give offence—I ask pardon of you, the captain, sir, and the other officers—having a good record until now—never been brought to the gangway—always done my best, as all my messmates will swear—was well and religiously brought up, never to drink overmuch or use bad language—can't think what came over me, being never in trouble before. . . .' Bascomb babbled on despairingly but the stream of apology finally dried up.

'Have you anything else to say?' asked Captain Trollope without intentional irony. Bascomb shook his head and closed his eyes with a shudder. Then came the order which was itself a rejection of the appeal:

'Strip.' Bascomb's shirt was pulled off him by the ship's corporal and he was dragged forward to the gratings, from which the blood was being wiped by a ship's boy. At this point Bascomb began to shriek his protests again, the torrent of words being indistinguishable. He was thrust into position and his arms forcibly extended.

'Seize him up,' ordered the captain and the two quartermasters deftly secured his struggling wrists. One of them pushed the leather bit into his mouth, ending his shrieks of protest.

'Seized up, sir,' a quartermaster reported.

Captain Trollope again produced his copy of *The Articles of War*, removed his hat (all others present doing the same) and read again the relevant Articles. This done, the next order should have been 'Do your duty,' but there was an unexpected interruption. The boatswain came forward and said:

'Beg pardon, sir. This man's messmates have offered to stand surety for him, asking you to stop their grog for a month if this man should again use abusive language to a superior officer.'

'Let one of his messmates stand forward.' An able seaman called Cookson came before the captain and said:

'We'll answer for Tom, sir, like the boatswain said.'

There was a pause of some seconds while the captain considered this idea as if it were entirely new to him. Then he appeared to make up his mind:

'Very well, your surety is accepted. Cut him down. Bascomb, you can return to duty. Ship's company, dismiss!'

Bascomb never even heard the words of reprieve, having

fainted. He was carried below and was never seen at the gratings again.

'I think that meets the case, sir,' said Delancey to the captain. 'Bascomb will have no influence after that exhibition of cowardice.'

'I agree,' said Captain Trollope, 'that did more good than a flogging would have done.' And there was no hint of mutiny in the *Glatton* after that.

There came a sudden and unseasonable change in the weather. September should ordinarily have been a month of calm seas and autumn skies but the weather broke on September 2nd with a rising gale from the northwest. Had mere safety been the object, Duncan could have run southward, quitting his station, but that would have left the Dutch fleet free to sail when the gale abated. So he stood his ground, beating to windward under short canvas until such time as the weather should improve. Far from improving, however, the gale blew harder than ever. Sail was further reduced but the ships were now making too much leeway. They ended up close to the Dutch coast, anchored in shallow water and hoping devoutly that their ground tackle would stand the strain. The sound of the gale rose to a shriek and by September 4th old seamen were using the word 'hurricane' to describe it. All the ships laboured heavily but perhaps the most uncomfortable of them all was the *Glatton* with her peculiarly heavy armament. Anchored as she was, the former Indiaman was bound to pitch but she now developed a new and violent roll. It became difficult and dangerous to move around the decks and all but impossible to sleep. She had been stripped to the lower masts at an early stage of the gale but that, while a help in one way, added to the stiffness caused by the weight of her lower deck carronades. She rolled jerkily and Delancey feared for the shrouds and stays.

At nearly the height of the gale on September 4th the *Monarch*, Onslow's flagship, made the signal to *Glatton* 'ACTS 27. verse 28.'

The signal midshipman had the bible open in an instant and read, 'And sounded and found twenty fathoms and when they had gone a little further they sounded again and found fifteen fathoms.'

'For God's sake!' shouted the master, but Delancey was at hand and grabbed the bible.

'Acknowledge,' he said, 'and reply as follows: HEBREWS 12 verse 6.'

Looking at the place, the master read 'For whom the Lord loveth He chasteneth . . .' As an answer it was at least adequate and Delancey was glad that he had marked the place, noting a text which might be generally useful.

The *Glatton* was in no great danger from the gale itself, for dismasting would not, of necessity, mean the loss of the ship. It would be a different story, however, if the guns were to snap their breaching ropes. Later on the 4th the gunner came to Delancey and reported his fears about the 68-pounders.

'If one gets loose, sir,' he yelled, cupping his hands, 'it'll go through the ship's side.'

They all had double breachings, as Delancey knew, and there was nothing more they could do.

'Have spare sails ready,' was all he could say, guessing that the gunner would long since have provided them. When a truck gun broke loose it was 'smothered' with a spare jib or stunsail. These 68-pounders were not on wheels (thank God) but would be hideously dangerous without that.

Later that day but still in daylight there came a scream and hubbub from the lower deck. Delancey scrambled below, clutching at the lifelines that had been rigged, and saw that there was chaos amidships.

'What's happened?' he shouted. 'Is there a gun loose?'

'No, sir,' bawled the boatswain. 'It's the *shot!*'

Delancey instantly knew what had happened and cursed himself inwardly for not providing against it. The shot for immediate use were ranged round the hatchways, each sunk into a circular hollow made in the timber, quite enough in the ordinary way to keep it there. But there was nothing ordinary about this tempest and nothing ordinary about the *Glatton*'s ammunition. Two of the 68-pound shot had been dislodged, he found, and had rolled across the deck. A seaman's leg had been broken before the shots had been jammed in a corner and it was lucky that no worse damage had been done.

Delancey had to think quickly. A 68-pound ball was impossibly heavy to handle. Rolling about the deck, it could be lethal. Falling down a hatchway, it could go through the ship's bottom. And where two had been dislodged there was no reason to think that the rest would stay in place. Delancey made a plan for lashing booms in place to keep the cannon balls from rolling but he was joined by Captain Trollope before he had time to give the necessary orders.

'We'll have all those shot in the hold,' yelled the captain. 'Put each in a bag made of doubled sailcloth and lower it with a tackle.'

'Aye, aye, sir,' said Delancey, and detailed the men to their different tasks.

It was a difficult and dangerous operation, with the ship plunging wildly, and there were a lot of minor injuries before the work was done. It was dark before Delancey could report completion and assure the captain that the 68-pound shot were all where they could fall no lower. It is quite possible that Trollope's solution was the right one—in so far at least as there could be any right solution—but the immediate effect was to lower the ship's centre of gravity. It could have made only a very small difference but a point of strain had been reached at which even small changes can count. The roll became worse and the mizzen mast rolled clean overboard. There followed a night-mare hour of frenzied effort in which two men lost their lives, washed over the stern, and three more were injured. It was midnight when the quarter-deck had been put to rights and then the foremast went over the side. This actually eased the ship's motion but left her little more than a floating wreck with huge seas breaking over her forecastle.

On the following day the wind, backing to south-west, became a mere half-gale and eventually no more than a breeze. Duncan's fleet had not lost a ship but had sustained damage enough to keep the men busy for the next week. In easily the worst state was the *Glatton* but Trollope was not the man to admit defeat. Admiring him before, Delancey was to confess afterwards that he admired Trollope more than ever during the next few days. The captain was everywhere, always active and encouraging, always knowing what to do next.

'Not that way!' he would shout. 'Bend a tackle to the forestay and lift with that.' 'Five more men tail on to this!'

The main yard became a new foremast, the fore yard a new mizzen, sails were swapped round and cordage spliced. The *Glatton* was soon under sail again, effective but ungainly, damaged but surviving. There was never a moment when a signal from the flagship had to be answered with the signal for inability. In what seems an incredibly short period of time, Duncan had his fleet once more in compact formation and ready for battle. The blockade of the Texel had never been lifted and the Dutch fleet had never been left unwatched.

On September 24th Captain Trollope was ordered by signal to go aboard the flagship. Duncan received him kindly and congratulated him on the speed with which the *Glatton*'s damage had been made good. With the admiral was Captain Brereton, a stranger to the fleet who had just arrived in a victualling hoy.

'I may tell you in confidence, gentlemen, that the recent gales proved too much for Captain Forster of the *Russell*. He has

asked to be relieved on the ground of ill-health. His first lieutenant, who is scarcely younger, has made a similar request. I
advised the Admiralty to post you, Captain Trollope, to the
Russell and send a replacement for you in the *Glatton*, which I am
sending into Portsmouth. Forster will go home in the hoy which
brought Captain Brereton to join us. Captain Trollope will take
command of the *Russell*, Captain Brereton will command the
Glatton. If you gentlemen agree with the arrangement, I propose
that Delancey goes as first lieutenant to the *Russell* and that the
second lieutenant of the *Glatton* should be promoted first. Are
we agreed?'

'Thank you, sir,' said Trollope, 'but Delancey is acting not
substantive first lieutenant of the *Glatton*. The appointed first
lieutenant is Mr Grant who—but you will remember the case,
sir.'

'Yes, of course,' said Admiral Duncan.

'Well, sir, I should like to continue the same arrangement in
the *Russell*, Grant to have the substantive post with Delancey
taking his place for the time being.'

'Isn't that a little unfair to Delancey?'

'I submit, sir, that any other arrangement would be unfair to
Grant.'

'I see what you mean. Very well, then. Delancey is to have the
acting appointment and Pringle is to be first in the *Glatton*. I
mustn't detain you, Captain Trollope, because you and
Delancey will have much to do before Captain Brereton can assume command of the *Glatton*. Your task, Captain Brereton, is a
simpler one and I shall ask you to remain for a little while. I
hope that you will both dine with me today before the *Glatton*
parts company.'

Trollope withdrew after accepting the invitation and the Admiral had a further talk with Brereton, explaining the peculiar
nature of the *Glatton*'s armament.

'The drawback is that the armament and ammunition,

which is not equally effective in every situation, is too heavy for the ship. I was seriously alarmed for the *Glatton* during the recent bad weather. I thought she might well be lost. Trollope saved her by a splendid feat of seamanship and I should never have interfered with the experiment while he remained in command. But now the moment has come to make some changes. You will take the *Glatton* to Portsmouth, together with my report on her qualities and defects and a separate letter to the Board of Ordnance. New guns will mean some structural alterations and a new establishment. Altogether, you must expect to spend some months in the dockyard. You should end with a ship less formidable in theory and a great deal safer in practice. Do not interpret anything I have said as a criticism of Captain Trollope. He is a brilliant officer for whom I have the greatest respect. But it won't do to have a ship that only a brilliant officer can command.'

Brereton, a solid and conventional man, was a good choice for the task of reducing the *Glatton* to a tame normality. Trollope himself had come to recognise the need for rearming the ship but he was glad to leave the task to someone else. Duncan's solution was the right one and Delancey welcomed the prospect of serving in a man-of-war designed for the purpose, a regular third-rate of 74 guns. She was an old ship, he knew, built as long ago as 1764 and designed by Sir Thomas Slade. She had played no significant part in the mutiny and was thought to be well officered and manned. What was less acceptable was the idea that he should remain acting first lieutenant of the *Russell* while Pringle, his junior, should become substantive first lieutenant of the *Glatton*, admittedly a smaller ship. He uttered no complaint, however, realising that there was a big element of luck in these things. There might be a general engagement, for instance, while the *Glatton* was still in dock.

He was more immediately consoled by an invitation to dine that day with Admiral Duncan. It was arranged, he knew, as a

farewell party for Captain Forster. He would himself be an
insignificant guest among all the senior officers but it looked
like a small mark of favour or recognition. Or was there in it a
hint of sympathy? He guessed that the only other lieutenant
there, apart from Duncan's flag lieutenant, would be Forster's
first in the *Russell*, old Bates with his failing eyesight and perpe-
tual cold. He went on to think of practical problems, of the need
for a clean shirt and a laced cravat. Had he any white stockings
fit to wear in the Admiral's presence? He was bound to feel
small when surrounded with so much gold lace but he might
hope at least to look clean and tidy. His mind went back to similar but worse problems he had faced as a midshipman bidden to
dine with the captain.

It was a fine autumn afternoon when the *Glatton*'s boat
returned to the flagship. The different captains were being
piped aboard, the ship's band was playing 'Heart of Oak' and a
marine guard of honour was drawn up to receive Vice-Admiral
Onslow. Captain Trollope was greeted at the entry port by his
cousin, Major Trollope of the Royal Marines.

'Welcome aboard, sir. The family is well represented today
for George Trollope has joined the *Trident* as third and the Admiral has been kind enough to include him. Delancey? Your
servant, sir.'

The dinner party was a great success with a variety of dishes
and plenty of champagne. The farewell to old Forster was the
pretext but all knew that the campaign was nearly over. The
blockade had been maintained (more or less) through the
summer's crisis and it was now September 24th, too late in the
year for any enemy expedition that might have been planned.
Intelligence reports indicated that the French troops, once
ready to embark, had been dispersed again. Within a few days
the fleet would sail for Yarmouth, leaving a token force off the
Texel. With any luck there would be weeks in harbour with
soft bread, fresh milk, green vegetables and a chance to meet

sweethearts and wives. There was a buzz of cheerful conversation and Delancey sitting at the foot of the table between old Bates and young Trollope, found himself involved in a discussion about the Dutch Navy.

'It's a great pity they never came out,' said Bates, 'for I shall retire without ever taking part in a general engagement. But the battle, had there been one, would have been more of a massacre. The Dutch ships are all obsolete.'

'But, surely, sir, the Dutch have a great reputation as seamen,' objected young Trollope. 'They fought well in the battles of the last century.'

'Indeed they did,' Bates had to admit. 'But their ships are also of the last century. In shallow waters like these they have clung to small two-decked ships with 44 or 50 guns, suitable for the Dutch harbours but unfit to meet a 74 in action.'

'But our ships here are not our latest and best,' said Delancey.

'They are not,' Bates conceded, 'but think of the experience we have had! By now we know their coast better than they do.'

At this point the party was called to order by Duncan's flag lieutenant and the Admiral himself gave the loyal toast. The flag-captain gave the toast of 'Admiral Duncan and the North Sea Fleet'. This was presently followed by a toast to Captain Forster and Mr Bates, wishing them joy in their retirement. Forster replied with a tribute to the fleet in which he had been privileged to serve, commanded by their host with such distinction and avoided by the enemy with such care. Vice-Admiral Onslow then gave the toast of 'The Trollope family!' which was greeted by laughter. Henry Trollope replied by explaining how unworthy he was to succeed Forster in command of the *Russell*. He ended by giving a toast to Captain Brereton, his own successor in the *Glatton*. She was still afloat, he added, much to everyone's surprise, but rumour had reached him that she was to be armed in future with muskets only. There was laughter and applause at this and there was a final toast to the Dutch Admiral '. . . and may he pluck up courage before the year ends!' It was altogether a pleasant and convivial occasion.

As they rowed back to the *Glatton* for the last time, Trollope spoke again about what chance remained of fighting the Dutch.

'The enemy have at least 16 sail of the line and there was at one time a French army of 30,000 men. In April the rumour was of an intended attack on Jersey or Guernsey. In June all the talk was of the threat to Ireland and the troops were at one time actually embarked. Well, nothing came of it despite the mutiny. It is September now, almost too late for any conjunct expedition, and the Admiral thinks that the French plan, whatever it may have been, has been cancelled. He means to fall back on Yarmouth at the end of the month.'

'And none too soon if I may say so. The fleet has been at sea for 18 weeks!'

'But the Admiral himself has been on this station for two years, almost without setting foot ashore!'

'I can't think, sir, how a man of his age can stand it.'

'Nor can I. Not that I know his exact age, but his flag lieutenant mentioned to me that the Admiral had gone down with a tropical complaint after the capture of Havana. That would have been in 1762 and he already a captain. . . . I should guess that he must be aged 65 or thereabouts.'

'And well-connected, sir, I have been told?'

'He married a niece of Henry Dundas. He'll not haul down his flag until he feels inclined. But the question is whether he will have a chance to fight the Dutch. He knows by now that the odds are against it.'

'What motive could the Dutch have, sir, for putting to sea?'

'None that I can see. Should there be an engagement, by the way, the Admiral's opponent will be Admiral de Winter. He is Dutch but has served in the French army, rising to the rank of General. Although he began in the Dutch Navy, he never so

much as commanded a ship. The Admiral says that De Winter
has been very gentlemanly in his behaviour. They have been in
correspondence, of course, over matters arising from our blockade.'

'When the Admiral goes to Yarmouth Roads or the Nore, he
will, I suppose, leave someone to mount guard here on the
Dutch coast?'

'He will indeed. And I can tell you now, in strict confidence,
that this will be my task. I have been given command of a small
squadron which will keep watch on the Texel and send warning
to the Admiral if the Dutch show themselves.

'Congratulations, sir. If we didn't know the Broad Four-
teens already, this would be our chance to make their better acquaintance.'

'We'll know them well enough before we have finished.'

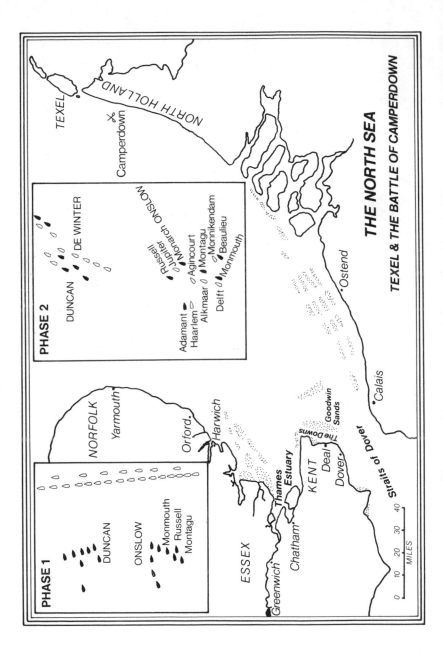

THE NORTH SEA

TEXEL & THE BATTLE OF CAMPERDOWN

☆ ☆

CHAPTER FIVE

Camperdown

TROLLOPE'S squadron of observation comprised the Russell (74), the *Adamant* (50), the *Circe* frigate (28) and three cutters, *Speculator, Vestal* and *Active*. Sailing from Yarmouth on October 3rd and leaving the Admiral there, Trollope sent the *Speculator* into the harbour mouth, watched by the *Circe*, which was again in sight of the *Russell*. There began a vigil which might have lasted the whole winter but actually ended on the 7th. The days of waiting were brought to a close by a signal from the *Speculator*, relayed by the *Circe*, that the enemy fleet was coming out of harbour and heading south-westerly. All that could be seen from the *Russell* was the *Circe* approaching under all sail with the *Speculator* beyond. As soon as they reported, Trollope sent off the *Speculator* with a despatch for the Commander-in-Chief at Yarmouth, the *Vestal* being sent to Lowestoft with a despatch for the Admiralty. Shadowed by the *Active* and watched at longer range by the *Circe*, the Dutch fleet was at first in some disorder but eventually assumed a more or less regular formation and continued slowly on course as if for the Channel. Further seaward, the *Russell* and *Adamant* kept in touch but still without sight of the enemy. Trollope sent for his officers, gathered them round his table and showed them the situation on the chart.

'Now, gentlemen, we know where Admiral de Winter is and we know that he has with him 16 sail of the line, five frigates and some smaller vessels. He has no transports and there is no reason to suppose that any troops have embarked. If his object had been to take part in some invasion plan he would most probably have headed in the opposite direction, meaning to go north-about, and yet I cannot suppose that he means to fight his way through the Straits of Dover with the North Sea Fleet at his heels and the Channel Fleet in front of him. What then does he hope to achieve? I shall be glad to have your ideas, gentlemen.'

The first to speak was the second lieutenant, a red-haired Scotsman called McTaggart:

'I'd surmise, sir, that he means to give battle, hoping that Admiral Duncan's fleet may have suffered some losses during the recent storm.'

'That is my opinion too,' said Vernon, the third lieutenant; 'and in fact we have been weakened by the *Glatton*'s return to port.'

'What do you think, Delancey?'

'Well, sir, I am remembering the cutter *Nancy* which we sent into the Texel under a flag of truce. I talked the other day with her master, Mr Terence O'Neill. He saw the Dutch ships and counted their gun ports and swears that they have only five ships of 74 guns. Their two-decked ships may number 16 but seven of them have fewer than 60 guns, several no more than 44. Ships in that class did well enough under Tromp and De Ruyter but they are not fit for the line of battle today. Of this fact the Dutch Admiral must be aware. It could not be *his* decision to give battle.'

'You mean that he is under orders?'

'Yes, sir. I suspect that the Dutch politicians and their French masters have no idea of their fleet's relative weakness.'

'So their Admiral will go about and head back for harbour?'

'That is my guess, sir. The Dutch can then boast that their fleet has been at sea but that the cowardly British avoided battle!'

'So it rests with us to bring about the general engagement which Admiral de Winter would like to prevent. It is now the 7th. With any luck Admiral Duncan should have the news in two days and make contact with us in two days after that—say, the 11th. We must shadow the Dutch in the meanwhile but keep out of sight.'

All the Dutch saw during the next three days was the one cutter. Her signals were received by the *Circe* and hers again by the *Russell*. On the 10th came the signal that Delancey had foreseen. The Dutch fleet had tacked in succession and was on its way back to port. Trollope now made closer contact with the enemy, watching anxiously for a first glimpse of Duncan's fleet. If all went well the Dutch and British fleets should be converging with Trollope's squadron between them. It was a question, however, whether Duncan could have put to sea quickly enough, several of his ships being in need of repair. Captain Trollope was in a fever of anxiety, pacing the deck or plotting the enemy position on the chart.

The hours of daylight on the 11th seemed eternal but Delancey, for one, determined not to waste them. He checked and double-checked on every arrangement, making sure that everyone had a pre-arranged successor.

'The Dutch will stand to their guns,' he told the gun captains. 'See to it that we fire three broadsides to their two.'

Then he checked again on fire precautions. 'There are flames there at the break of the forecastle. What do you do? And what do you do after that?' Now was the time, he explained, to think ahead.

For Delancey the momentous day of October 12th began at daybreak with the enemy fleet in sight. The sky was overcast, the light poor and the wind blowing strong from the north-east. It changed presently, however, and, backing, turned into a westerly breeze.

'Well, there's the enemy,' said Captain Trollope. 'Where's our Admiral?'

'I think that the *Circe* is in touch, sir,' replied Delancey, telescope focussed.

'Thank God for that. Yes, she is signalling the enemy numbers. We'll pipe all hands to breakfast as soon as possible and then clear for action.'

'Aye, aye, sir.'

Delancey gave the necessary orders and had the guns run out and secured. Carpenters dismantled all the cabins, beginning with that of the captain. Servants carried furniture and sea chests down to the hold, with lamps and curtains rolled in the rugs. Canvas screens were rolled up and tied to the deck beams. Wooden partitions fell apart and disappeared as if by magic. The cockpit was turned into the operating theatre, with the midshipman's chests covered by an old piece of canvas. The decks were sanded and the tubs of water appeared between the cannon. Cartridges appeared for immediate use and each gunlock was checked and tested. The men forming each gun's crew stripped to the waist and each man tied a kerchief round his head to cover the ears and deaden the sound of gunfire. Marines were posted at their stations, each musket inspected, each flintlock examined. Then, after making a quick inspection of the decks Delancey reported the ship ready for battle. Captain Trollope then carried out his own more leisurely inspection, having a word here and there with the gun captains and other petty officers. He lingered a little over the carronades, telling the men that the Dutch were without them.

'The Dutch will fight, my lads, make no mistake about that. It won't be like fighting the French or Spanish. But we mount a heavier broadside than the enemy. We'll beat them! We'll make them wish they were back in Amsterdam! Fire low and shoot to kill!'

Back on the quarterdeck, Delancey could now see both fleets

without a telescope. The Dutch were forming line as they headed back towards the Texel. Duncan was coming up before the westerly wind, the *Circe* and *Speculator* signalling back information and the *Russell* and *Adamant* ready to take their place in the line.

'I can't for the life of me see what the Dutch are doing. Why should they have come out at all?'

'Perhaps to give battle, sir?'

'Why in that case should they run for home?'

'I wonder, sir, whether they are not trying to lure us into danger on a lee shore?'

'If that is their plan it is madness. Theirs is a fleet that has never been to sea, led by an Admiral who has never so much as commanded a ship. Ours is a fleet that has been blockading the Texel for two years. Our ships may be worn out—and this one, for example, is about due to be broken up—but we know their coast better than they do. Our difficulty will be one of time. The Dutch may be back in harbour before our line of battle is even formed. I hope to God the Admiral does not waste time over that. You were right, Delancey, about the Dutch ships. I have been studying them with a telescope. They may be two-decked but some of them are no bigger than our 38-gun frigates and one of them could be smaller. Their chance in a modern battle is that of a snowball in hell. We shall feel sorry for them when the battle is actually joined; sorrier still before it is over.'

Duncan's fleet was coming up under all sail with top-gallants set. There could be no more impressive sight in the world, that cluster of well-ordered and disciplined men-of-war, not formed in order of battle but all working together and inspired by a single purpose. The fleet formed two groups, the more northerly led by Duncan himself in the *Venerable*, the more southerly led by Vice-Admiral Onslow. The *Circe* was now racing westwards, close-hauled, with the purpose of giving Duncan the fullest information about the enemy. Captain Trollope steered so as to join Onslow's division of the fleet, to which both the *Russell* and *Adamant* belonged. There was no attempt at an exact formation and the *Russell* eventually joined what was merely a group of nine ships, heading for the rear half of the Dutch line. Soon after half-past ten the flagship made the signal for a 'General Chase'.

'Well done!' exclaimed Captain Trollope. 'The Admiral means to attack at once without waiting to form line. The Dutch can't escape now!'

There were 16 ships on either side, and it was obvious that Duncan meant to break the Dutch line and engage their ships from to leeward, much as Nelson had done at the Battle of the Nile. This intention was confirmed by signal at midday, by which time battle was imminent. The *Russell* was to starboard of Onslow's flagship *Monarch* with only the *Montagu* beyond her again. The scene from the *Russell* was grimly impressive and Delancey, looking about him, reflected that years of discipline and training were now to be put to the test. If he and the other lieutenants had done their work properly, the *Russell* would fire three broadsides in the time needed by the Dutch to fire two. The fight would be at close range and the casualties would be heavy on either side. The French often used to fire at their opponents' masts and rigging but the Dutch would never do that. They would fire low and fire accurately.

Delancey shivered involuntarily, feeling very exposed on the open deck. Of one thing he felt sure, that the men were in good heart. Still more to the point, they were eager to make amends for the recent mutiny. Ships foremost in the troubles at the Nore had been said at the time to be manned by cowards. These, after all, were the men who had left Duncan to blockade the Texel almost single-handed. They were intent now on redeeming their reputation. As for the Dutch, Delancey knew that their officers would have been reminding them of past glories, telling them once more about Tromp and De Ruyter. But what could they do with a fleet which had never been exercised on target practice, let alone in action? The way things were going, Onslow was going to overwhelm their rear, bringing nine ships to bear against five. Duncan was going to overwhelm their leading ships, leaving the Dutch centre unopposed. There would be some hard fighting—no doubt of that—but the Dutch were going to be annihilated.

The battle began at half-past twelve when the Dutch *Jupiter* fired at the *Monarch*.

'Look at that!' said Captain Trollope, 'Onslow hasn't even replied! He'll rake the *Jupiter* with his first broadside—you'll see.'

A few minutes later the *Monarch* passed astern of the *Jupiter* (flying a rear-admiral's flag) and ahead of the next ship. She raked them both with simultaneous broadsides.

'A good beginning!' said the captain. 'That's *our* opponent.' He pointed to the last ship but one, leaving the last of all to the *Montagu*.

Firing was now general and the scene confused by smoke but Trollope held his fire and presently bore up to avoid a collision. The final result was to place the last Dutch ship, the *Delft*, between the *Russell* and the *Montagu*; a 50-gun ship trapped between two 74's.

'Fire!' shouted Trollope, and the *Russell*'s starboard broadside thundered.

The port broadside of the *Montagu* crashed out a minute afterwards, beginning that murderous cross-fire by which the *Delft* was almost literally torn to pieces. The Dutchmen stood to their guns and the *Russell* sustained some casualties in the first few minutes, but the drill for fighting both broadsides was complex and the crew of the *Delft* were all too unpractised.

Delancey was sickened by what he saw and Captain Trollope evidently felt the same about it. Shouting to make himself heard, the captain said: 'Why don't they strike?'

'Why indeed?' Delancey could see the *Delft* when the smoke blew aside from the *Russell*'s quarterdeck carronades. Amidships, some three of the *Delft*'s gun-ports had become one, the timbers which separated them being shattered into wreckage. She looked at that point like an old barrel staved in by an angry boot. Further aft some men were trying to extinguish a fire at the foot of the mizzen mast. A burning sail had fallen across the bitts and at least one man was trapped under it, his screams being just audible through the general tumult. On the Dutch quarterdeck two guns had overturned, one of them on top of a bloodstained corpse. A third gun had burst, killing or wounding the entire gun's crew. One man had been blown in half, another had lost both arms, a third had lost his leg. There was blood everywhere and fragments of mutilated limbs. It looked as if some half-trained gunner had applied the match before the cannon ball had been rammed home. How often had he warned seamen against that? The *Russell*'s men would not make that sort of mistake, not even in the heat of battle, but what chance had those Dutchmen? They had never been properly exercised at sea. Few of them had been in action before. What they had now to face was not battle but murder. God—that man under the burning sail was still alive. . . .

'Fire!' came the sound of a midshipman's voice and the whole grisly scene was mercifully blotted out by smoke. There was a crash somewhere forward in the *Russell* where a spar had fallen. A minute later the sailing master, standing near the wheel, pitched forward on his face in a pool of blood. He had been hit in the shoulder by a musket ball, probably aimed at the helmsman. As he was taken to the cockpit, a master's mate took his place and received a musket ball through his hat. Some marines returned the fire, on Delancey's orders, and the Dutch marksman was silenced. With the smoke blown aside the *Delft* was once more visible and her plight was now worse. The *Montagu* fired into her from the opposite side, wrecking her forecastle and dismounting three more of her quarterdeck guns. What was happening between decks could only be guessed but her waist must look like a mere slaughterhouse.

'Fire!' came the boy's voice and the scene was once more hidden in smoke.

'Why don't they strike?' asked Trollope angrily and then added: 'I can't stand this any longer. She's crippled now. Make sail again—we'll find another opponent.'

Delancey shouted the necessary orders and men raced up the rigging. Sails were let fall and the *Russell* began slowly to draw away. The sound of gunfire lessened as she sailed past the shattered *Alkmaar*, went to windward of the *Powerful* and *Adamant*, glimpsed the *Agincourt* (which seemed to be avoiding battle) and ended up engaging the *Jupiter*, a 74-gun ship with a vice-admiral's flag. It looked for a moment as if a duel might follow on more equal terms but Trollope then realised that the *Jupiter* was simultaneously under fire from the *Monarch*, Onslow's flagship. She hauled down her flag at 1.45, one vice-admiral surrendering to another, and the *Russell* moved away. Looking astern, Delancey could see that three other Dutch ships had surrendered and that the *Delft* was a floating wreck. Nearest to the *Russell* at that moment was another Dutch ship, the *Wassenaer*, and she had already surrendered. To the north-east, at some little distance and hidden by smoke a separate battle was raging round De Winter's flagship. Delancey heard the gunfire but knew little of what had happened until afterwards. The leading Dutch ships had been as decisively beaten, only seven of them making their escape and three flag officers, De Winter one of them, being compelled to surrender. The last service performed by the *Russell* was in sending her boats to the rescue of the *Delft*'s crew, many of whom were saved before the ship actually sank.

The firing died away during the afternoon, leaving both fleets tossing uneasily in a rough sea and a rising wind. Some of the

Dutch ships had escaped in the failing light, the rest were scattered or sinking hulks, saved with difficulty or left to go ashore on the shoals to leeward. The Dutch coast was only five miles distant and the ships were in only nine fathoms of water. The casualties in the *Russell* were relatively few, none killed and only seven wounded; those hurt including Lieutenant Johnson and the master, a master's mate, the boatswain and a sergeant of marines. The damage to hull and rigging was considerable and Delancey had no easy task in carrying out the necessary repairs, the knotting and splicing and patching which would enable the ship to claw her way to safety and eventually reach the Nore.

It was hard work for all, made no easier for want of the master and boatswain, and Delancey breathed a sigh of relief when he finally gave the order to drop anchor. It was not until dinner time on the following day that the officers had the leisure to discuss the battle. In the aftermath their mood was surprisingly sombre.

'I suppose,' said Vernon, 'that this was the first battle for most of us—I mean, the first general engagement. I'll confess that it has left me with a sense of disappointment.'

'I know,' said Lloyd, 'it was not so much a conflict as a massacre. It is a question, to begin with, why the Dutch fleet should have left harbour at all. De Winter seems to have had no object in view. The talk at one time had been of invading Ireland, but that was all over and the troops had disembarked. The Dutch sortie seems to have been pointless.'

'I learn from the captain,' said Delancey, 'that De Winter had orders to sail—orders from the Dutch Admiralty. Some of their civilians thought that he would repeat the Dutch exploits of the last century.'

'Well, why not?' said Lloyd. 'He had ships which dated from the last century. Take that wretched ship we engaged at the outset.'

'The *Delft*,' Delancey put in.

'Yes, the *Delft*. She should never have been in the line of battle.'

'But we have 50-gun ships too,' objected McClure, the surgeon, 'there's the *Adamant*—yes, and the *Chatham*.'

'The type is obsolete, for all that,' Lloyd insisted, 'and the *Chatham* was built as long ago as 1758! A 50-gun ship can be useful as peacetime flagship on a foreign station or sometimes as escort to a convoy. But to put such a ship in the line of battle is murder.'

'Against a 74-gun ship, I agree,' said McClure.

'But the *Delft*,' said Lloyd, 'found herself between us and the *Montagu*. We shall never know how many of her men were killed or wounded for most of those wounded were afterwards drowned. When Bullen of the *Monmouth* was rescued from her he said afterwards that the state of the *Delft* was unbelievable. She was nothing more than a blood-stained shambles.'

'I wonder that she kept firing for as long as she did,' Delancey observed. 'These Dutch ships had never been under fire before.'

'The Dutch stood well to their guns,' said McClure, 'as some of our messmates will have to admit. But I should suppose that many of their men were disaffected, having no love for republicans, whether French or Dutch. Some of their ships in the centre deserted the rest.'

'We shall do poorly in prize-money,' said Lloyd finally; 'the captured ships we have brought in are all but worthless.'

This prediction about prize-money turned out to be all too accurate. The prizes could only be valued as firewood, no single one of them being taken into the service. The victors of Camperdown did not, however, go unrewarded. News came of a peerage for Admiral Duncan, who thus became Baron Duncan of Lundie and Viscount Duncan of Camperdown. It was also announced that the fleet was to be visited by King George III himself. This was to be on October 30th, for which occasion

some elaborate preparations were made. Captain Trollope sent
for Delancey beforehand and told him that the *Russell* would be
under his command for the next few days.

'The plan is for His Majesty to drive down to Greenwich
Hospital and embark there in the *Royal Charlotte* yacht. There
are to be two other yachts as well, the *Princess Augusta* and the
Mary, the former to accommodate the Lords Commissioners of
the Admiralty. I am to command the *Royal Charlotte* on this occasion.'

'Congratulations, sir.'

'Congratulate me when the whole affair is over. The chances
are that the weather will be adverse. If I wreck the yacht and
drown our sovereign I shall spend the rest of my life explaining
the disaster.'

'I am sure that all will go well, sir. As for their Lordships,
they will be visiting the Nore under very different conditions—as compared, I mean, with their last visit.'

'Egad, that's true. The same ships that were in a state of
mutiny a few months ago are back again with 11 enemy ships
taken and three captured admirals.'

'It says much, sir, for Admiral Duncan's leadership.'

'Indeed it does. And now I leave you to make the *Russell* fit for
the King's inspection.'

There followed some days of furious activity, with carpentry
and re-rigging gradually giving place to painting and polishing,
the officers subscribing to buy gold leaf for the figurehead and
stern carving, the petty officers doing the same for the top-
gallant masthead caps. Rehearsals followed in manning ship
and receiving distinguished guests.

All was ready on October 30th but the day brought with it a
stiff easterly breeze which freshened until it was blowing half a
gale. 'The *Royal Charlotte* will never make it,' said Delancey to
himself while continuing with active preparations. All other ex-
perienced seamen said the same but all went on with their

work. Only in the afternoon did the signal come that the royal visit was cancelled. The King had reached Gravesend but had then turned back, finally landing again at Greenwich. It was a sad anticlimax and Delancey felt that something had to be said by somebody. When the ship's company was assembled he made what was almost his first effort at public speaking:

'We expected to have His Majesty with us today, coming down river in the *Royal Charlotte* from Greenwich. The wind has been adverse and I have now been told that the *Royal Charlotte* has had to turn back. When you realise that Captain Trollope was in command of the royal yacht you will agree with me that the voyage, if possible, would have been performed. With neither the King present nor Captain Trollope, it falls to me to say what each would have said on this occasion had he been here. Captain Trollope would have said, "Well done, lads. Our ship has battled the watch for a third of a century. She has just been in a major action. You have made her look as if she had just been launched!" And His Majesty? He would have said what I say now: "All hands, splice the mainbrace!"' There were cheers at this and the grog was issued.

Delancey later supplied the wine for the wardroom dinner, by which hour the news had come that Captain Trollope had been knighted by the King before he disembarked at Greenwich. This enabled Delancey to propose the toast to Sir Henry Trollope, 'but for whose courage and seamanship the Battle of Camperdown would never have been fought.'

He was a little taken aback when Vernon followed this up with a toast to, 'Captain Delancey—with congratulations from all his messmates on his well-deserved promotion.'

Delancey interrupted him smartly at that, saying, 'Come, gentlemen, we know nothing about promotion for anybody. Our toast should be to our shipmates, the petty officers, seamen and marines of the *Russell*.'

On the following day Delancey went ashore and revisited the

Golden Cockerel, where he was greeted by his old friends, 'Crowbar' Crowley, Dumbell and Wetherall. They all wished him well on his coming promotion but he told them to wait until they saw his name in the Gazette.

'Ah,' said Crowley, 'that reminds me. There was something in today's newspaper which you ought to see. What was it now?'

'Blowed if I know,' said Wetherall, 'but I have the newspaper here and you can see for yourself.'

Crowley took the newspaper, put on his spectacles and began to search through the columns.

'Maybe it was an obituary, recording the death of an old officer, promoted for gallantry but never employed again. What was his name now? Otway? Hockley? But I can't find any obituary here—not a single one. On the second page they are, sometimes, but I do believe that they have been crowded out today by the report from Maidstone Quarter Sessions. There is the verdict, you see, on that farmer who killed the dairy-maid—a shocking case. I daresay that she was a tiresome girl but that was no excuse for snatching up a billhook and—disgraceful, I call it, and so messy, it seems. Ah, here it is! Here is the news you should know about: "Naval lieutenant acquitted of murder." Yes, this is it. Listen, all of you: "Mr Alexander Grant of His Majesty's ship *Glatton*, accused of murdering Thomas Batley, serving on board the same ship, was yesterday acquitted on the ground that the said Thomas Batley was mutinous and associated with others who were in a state of mutiny. The case was dismissed before any evidence for the defence was called, it being held that Mr Grant was justified in what he did and that there was no case to answer." I thought when I read that, Mr Delancey will be interested in this case because the *Glatton* was his ship, but then I forgot about it.'

'Thank you, Mr Crowley. It so happens that I am very interested indeed.'

☆ ☆

CHAPTER SIX

The Aftermath

CAPTAIN SIR HENRY TROLLOPE was in London for some weeks after receiving his knighthood. The North Sea Fleet was in harbour, its blockading duties at an end, and ceremonies, banquets and thanksgivings were the order of the day. In obedience to a letter from Sir Henry, Delancey came up to London, handing over command of the *Russell* to Vernon, and reported to the Admiralty. He was told that the King was to attend a special service at St Paul's, thanking God for the three naval victories gained respectively by Lord Howe, Lord St Vincent and Lord Duncan. The captured flags were to go through the streets on artillery waggons but were then to be carried into the cathedral by lieutenants who had taken part in the several engagements. Delancey was to be one of these and was briefed, with the others, by a minor court official called Paget. The first written directions were clear enough and a first rehearsal went off without a hitch. Then came the first amendment. The flags were to be arranged in a circle under the dome and each was then to be handed to an admiral. It was thereafter the admirals who would hand the flags to the Bishop of Lincoln (he was also Dean of St Paul's), whose task it would be to lay them on the altar. The general concept was appropriate but the difficulty was to collect the admirals together for a rehearsal. Each had a representative present at each briefing but it was not the representatives who would be present on the great day. Mr Paget hurried backward and forward between St James's Palace, the Admiralty, the Deanery and the College of Arms. The order of proceedings came to be written, amended, rewritten and revised, each flag-bearer coming to wish in the end that some other officer had been chosen for the honour.

For Delancey the effect of all this preparation was to keep him in London for several weeks, mildly occupied but free to spend each evening as he chose, having supper at a tavern or going to the play. The town was festive and each theatre had an illumination representing the Battle of Camperdown. There was even greater excitement when the rumour spread that Lord Duncan was himself in town. He had not so far been present at any rehearsal, Mr Paget sending successive directives to Walmer Castle, where he was known to be staying with the Prime Minister. His arrival in town solved one problem but created another because it could be assumed that the last directive was at Walmer. With a meeting tomorrow, the first at which his lordship would be present, the fussy Mr Paget was in despair. It was vital that the Admiral should have the outline plan beforehand. Delancey volunteered to deliver the letter that afternoon and his offer was eagerly accepted, all the regular messengers being already sent elsewhere.

'Very good of you, Mr Delancey—I am really most grateful. I understand that he is staying with his brother-in-law, Mr William Dundas, member of Parliament, at his lodging in Lincoln's Inn Fields.'

Delancey took the vital letter and set off in a hackney carriage for Lincoln's Inn. He found the right place but a servant told him that Mr Dundas had gone with a friend to dine at the Piazza Coffee House in Covent Garden. Guessing who the friend must be, Delancey told his driver to head for Covent Garden.

The Piazza was a large and well-known restaurant and crowded each day but the head waiter knew his clients. 'Mr

Dundas, sir? Nephew to Mr Secretary Dundas? This way, sir.'

He guided Delancey to one of the smaller tables at which two gentlemen were having beefsteak and a bottle of claret. The one was unknown to Delancey but the other, although in civilian clothes, was unmistakably the giant and burly Viscount Duncan of Camperdown.

'Mr Dundas, sir? Allow me to introduce myself as Richard Delancey, first lieutenant of the *Russell*. I have a letter for his lordship and have been asked to deliver it in person.'

'Glad to make your acquaintance, Mr Delancey. Pray join us in a glass of claret. I take it that you are already known to his lordship?'

'Your servant, sir,' said Lord Duncan. 'You were once my guest aboard the *Venerable* and Sir Henry speaks very highly of you.'

Delancey bowed low and handed over the letter, sitting down on a chair which a waiter had produced from nowhere.

'What's all this twaddle?' asked the Admiral after glancing at the long-winded directive. 'All this to tell me how to behave? There's one thing I've learnt about ceremonial occasions. Take no notice of the earlier instructions because they'll all be cancelled before the day itself! When I'm in the cathedral I'll ask what I have to do and if it maks no muckle sense I'll e'en follow the guid Scots advice of Captain Inglis in the recent battle 'Up wi' the hel-lem and gang into the middle o' it.'''

Neither Lord Duncan nor Delancey was in uniform but there was evidently a service air about their meeting. Within a few minutes Mr Dundas was handed a note sent him by an acquaintance who was dining at a few tables' distance. In it he asked whether Dundas's guest were not Lord Duncan? Dundas looked round and nodded in the right direction.

The result was unexpected and inconvenient. The gentleman to whom Dundas had nodded jumped on the table, glass in hand, and demanded that all present should drink the Admiral's health. This was done and Duncan said a word of thanks but this was followed by three cheers from all present and this again by pandemonium. Aided by Dundas and Delancey, the Admiral reached the door and signalled up a hackney coach, but this manoeuvre failed, for the bystanders removed the horses and dragged the coach round Covent Garden. Delancey then saved the situation by finding another coach and so Lord Duncan finally escaped. As this second vehicle disappeared, Delancey stood back, blundering into a gentleman who had been cheering with the rest of the crowd.

'I beg your pardon, sir,' he said, but found himself face to face with someone whose face looked familiar. He was himself half recognised at the same time and said, after a final effort of memory:

'Good god, sir—surely—is it possible?—Aren't you Oliver Delancey?' The gentleman addressed, a handsome man of military bearing, replied:

'And you are—but of course—young Richard Delancey, my naval cousin!'

'No longer so young, sir, but Richard nevertheless!'

'We haven't met for over ten years, and here we collide in a London street!'

'But I suppose your family moved here after the last war?—I heard some rumour of that.'

'Yes, America was no place for a loyalist family, least of all after we had lost our New York estates. Father lives in retirement at Bath. I am Colonel of the 17th Dragoons and barrack-master-general. My nephew William is captain in the 16th Light Dragoons, and he also is in touch. We must dine together and talk of old times.'

'And Charlotte?'

'A sad business . . . She married young Bayard and died in childbirth three years later. I had forgotten that—that you had been interested. Let's meet here at the Piazza to-morrow. Is that convenient for you? I shall ask William. At half-past three? Very well then. Goodbye until then!'

Richard Delancey walked away thinking over this chance meeting. It seemed a lifetime indeed since he had been a midshipman in New York, thinking himself in love with Charlotte Delancey. That was the only time of his life when he had seemed to be a member of good society. His relatives, he had discovered, were all American and they had accepted him, after some hesitation, as a cousin; poor and without prospects but still a Delancey. In Britain he was nobody, a Guernseyman of dubious origin. In Guernsey he had won some reputation among the privateeersmen but was not a true islander nor regarded as such. For a moment, at the Piazza, he had sat at the same table as Lord Duncan and Mr William Dundas, Member of Parliament for Edinburgh. He had thought then how wonderful it must be to belong, as they both did, to known and aristocratic families. His own name sounded well enough but he knew not a soul in London. The people who really mattered were all related to each other but his nearest relatives, as he had believed, were in New York. Now it seemed that they were all in England, still wealthy, still holding high military rank and still inclined to accept him as a poor relation. To have these dashing cavalrymen as kinsfolk was to be somebody in the world, more especially if he were promoted. He looked forward to meeting Oliver and William again. The invitation he had received made him feel less alone in the world.

Next day Delancey assured Mr Paget that Lord Duncan had been handed the latest order of proceedings. He was thanked rather absently and then told that he would not himself be wanted after all.

'Knowing that Mr Philips of the *Ardent* was to be promoted post-captain, I assumed that he would not be available to act as flag-bearer at the service of thanksgiving. It seems now that his promotion, although agreed, has not actually been gazetted. I was informed only yesterday that he can be present, which is of course highly desirable in view of the distinguished part he played in the battle.' This announcement was followed by a few words of thanks and consolation. Then Mr Paget bustled off, muttering something about a change in the time of arrival which would affect the order in which the waggons would assemble.

Half relieved and half disappointed, Delancey left the other officers to study the latest—but obviously not the final—set of instructions. He had no other business in London save to call on Sir Henry Trollope in St James's Street and report that he was no longer wanted at the thanksgiving service and would be returning to the *Russell*. Sir Henry being out, he left a note of explanation and returned to his lodging in Piccadilly, where he gave notice of his departure on the morrow. He then called at his tailor to be measured for a new uniform.

Old Mr Hollingworth fussed over him with a tape-measure and talked of gold lace, 'I noticed, sir, that you were first in the *Russell* at the recent battle. That means promotion and a different style of uniform. I can alter your old uniform to serve for daily use but you will need something better when dining with the Admiral or attending a Levee, something more in the current mode.' Delancey agreed to this but said that he would confirm the order when he saw his name in the gazette. He made a mental note concerning the new hat which he would need to go with the new uniform and was glad to think that his sword, at least, would pass muster. New shirts, stockings and cravat he felt justified in purchasing straight away as useful in any case. He knew that aristocratic captains would buy silver plate for their dining tables and that an admiral's plate, when he was appointed commander-in-chief, would cost about £2,000. He wisely decided to defer that sort of investment until his account with his agent looked more impressive. After the day's shopping he would still be in credit, he thought, but only just. For his stay in London he could claim on the Admiralty but it would be months, of course, before a penny would be paid. There would be head-money payable in respect of the enemy ships taken or sunk at Camperdown but this again would take time to recover, being useful in the meanwhile, however, as a basis for credit. He had made no prize-money since he joined the *Russell*.

The dinner at the Piazza Coffee House was excellent and Colonel Delancey was a charming host, very much the man of fashion. He and his nephew were in civilian dress but both, from their bearing, were obviously soldiers and William had even been addressed as 'Cap'n' by the man who opened his carriage door.

'I am rising fifty now,' Oliver explained 'and had my share of fighting in the last war. I do staff work these days, planning barracks everywhere. The family's next hero will be this fellow William. Any day we shall hear tell of his dragoons cutting their way through the French army. Waiter, refill the glasses! And what about you, Richard? Were you at the Battle of St Vincent?'

'No, sir. I fought under Lord Duncan's command in the recent engagement on the Dutch coast.'

'Did you, by God! And that was the bloodiest affair of the whole war, or so they say. Were you in the flagship?'

'No, sir, I was in the *Russell*, commanded by Captain Trollope, now Sir Henry.'

'And it was Trollope,' said William, 'who brought the battle about. A clever man if ever there was one! I met him t'other evening at Lady Sarah's.'

'And the *Russell*, I suppose, was in the thick of the fight?' asked the Colonel.

'Not really,' Richard replied. 'We were opposed by a wretched Dutch 50-gun ship called the *Delft*. She was a bloodstained bundle of firewood before we had finished with her. She hauled down her flag but sank before the prize-crew could bring her into port. We couldn't find another opponent after that—they had all surrendered or fled.'

'So you didn't have many casualties?' asked William.

'Seven wounded, no one killed.'

'That does you no credit at all,' said William. 'There are two rules of war, whether by land or sea. The first is that you gain more respect from one general engagement than from a dozen skirmishes in which you actually risk your life. You can now say "I was at Camperdown" and that makes you a hero even if no enemy shot came within a mile of you. My uncle here was at the Battle of Brooklyn and the Battle of White Plains—I don't suppose he killed anyone on either occasion—but was near to death in a dozen encounters nobody has ever heard about. It is the battles that have made him a veteran. The second rule of war is that you gain distinction in proportion to the number of men you lose. Blunder into an ambush, lose half your bloody regiment, have your horse shot under you and come in with a flesh wound—then you are a hero and fit to be a General!'

'You have forgotten the third rule,' said the Colonel. 'Keep your regiment out of serious trouble and you are put in charge of the barracks!'

There was laughter over this and then William asked Richard what his position was in the *Russell*.

'I am acting first-lieutenant.'

'Then you are due for promotion! We must drink your health as—what d'you call it?—Master and Commander. To Captain Richard Delancey!'

It was a very pleasant evening indeed. The two cavalrymen, uncle and nephew, shared the same careless and cynical manner. The older man had seen enough of the tented field and was very much a man about town. To be of any use as general in a given campaign it is essential, he explained, to have been trained in that war and not the previous one. His war had been in America and everything had changed since. The younger man had the same aristocratic mannerisms but a deeper interest in his profession. Both were full of oblique references to their fashionable friends, to 'Lord H' and 'Old Q', to Lady Harriet and young Katie. So far as birth went these Delanceys were no better connected than he was, but they had money and this was evidently the secret of making more.

'Let's see,' said the Colonel, 'you were brought up in Guernsey—so much I can remember. I think there should be the need for some more barracks there.'

'Very likely, sir. There are some barracks above St Peter Port.' Richard could picture them as he spoke. He had once fought a duel within sight of them.

'Yes, but what about the north of the island? We shall need some there if this war goes on much longer. They should be near—what's that village called, the one with a harbour?'

'St Sampson's, sir.'

'That's the place. I must study the map again.'

It seemed odd to Richard that the plan for more barracks in Guernsey should thus originate in London. He had supposed that the demand would come from the Lieutenant-Governor of Guernsey and run into opposition at the Horse Guards on the ground of needless expense. All this, however, was a military problem and far outside his experience.

The dinner over, he parted from his friends and relatives on very good terms, slept that night at his lodgings and set off next day in the coach for Rochester and Chatham. He was glad to be back in the *Russell*, if only to avoid further expense, and Vernon told him that Sir Henry was to be in London for the next few days but would return on the day after the service of thanksgiving at St Paul's. 'It is to be a tremendous occasion, I hear.'

'Yes, indeed,' said Delancey, rather shortly. He resumed

command and set about the training of some newly-joined replacements.

Sir Henry Trollope was cheered by the crew when he came aboard, as also by the men on board the nearer ships in the anchorage. Despite this, however, he looked worried and distressed. Sending for Delancey, he presently began:

'Perhaps you will have heard, Delancey, that the rewards allowed to the North Sea Fleet have been on a generous scale. A peerage for Admiral Duncan, a baronetcy for Admiral Onslow, a knighthood for Fairfax and myself, a free pardon to a number of mutineers and a medal for each of the captains. You may also have heard that each first lieutenant is to be promoted Master and Commander—except, by the way, for Phillips of the *Ardent* who is to be promoted post captain. You will realise, of course, that promotion of the first lieutenant is regarded as a compliment to the captain in each case. As promotion to rear-admiral is solely a matter of seniority, the captain who takes an enemy ship cannot be promoted. Promotion goes, therefore, to his right hand man, who may even (as in Philips' case) be made post captain without the intermediate step. The *Ardent*, by the way, was the ship which suffered the heaviest casualties—41 killed including the captain and another officer, 107 wounded including eight officers!—and it was Philips, as you know, who continued the action after Burgess was killed. You will also have heard, I expect, that Williamson of the *Agincourt* is to be court-martialled and you may think, as I do, that certain other officers are lucky to escape the same fate.'

During these first minutes Captain Trollope seemed to be postponing the revelation of something unpleasant, probably concerning Delancey's promotion. He came at length to the point:

'As regards the *Russell*, our situation was peculiar. Our appointed first lieutenant has been happily acquitted at Maidstone Quarter Sessions. It was you, however, the acting first lieutenant, who took a very creditable part in the battle. At the Admiralty I asked for you both to be promoted. This was refused. It was pointed out to me that other captains would ask why they should not equally have the right to make two promotions. It was also pointed out that the *Russell*, while playing her part, had not been in the worst of the fighting. In other words, our 'butcher's bill' was nothing like that of the *Ardent*. I can never see that heavy casualties are a proof of heroism—they often result from the captain's stupidity—but it is in these terms that merit is assessed at the Admiralty. No. I could have only the one promotion but the choice was left to me.

'You must realise that I was in a very difficult position. I have the highest opinion of you both. You both unquestionably deserve promotion. Grant is the best first lieutenant I have ever had, a brilliant officer, a perfectionist, an excellent disciplinarian. I would not say that you are quite his equal—forgive me for speaking plainly—but you did very well in battle; no one could have done more. Well, you can see my difficulty. I had to choose, and I chose Grant.'

After a pause, Captain Trollope went on:

'I want you to know why I made that choice. You will yourself remember what Grant did for the *Glatton*, a converted merchantman, a makeshift and nondescript man-of-war with an experimental armament. She was formidable before he had finished with her, a miniature ship of the line. I could never have done that without him.

'Grant is now a free man again, but with what sort of a future? Suppose he came back to the *Russell* as first lieutenant, you being replaced on promotion? People would say I had deliberately overlooked him in promoting you. He would be the man who had faced a court-martial and escaped on a technicality. There was no verdict of 'Not Guilty' so far as the Navy is concerned. What he needs is a sign from the Admiralty that he stands exonerated, that he was right to deal with mutiny in the way he did. There is only one way of publicly supporting his action and that is by promoting him. That is the complete answer to all whisperings and rumours. You may remember all that was said against Bligh following the mutiny on board the *Bounty*. To that the Admiralty's answer was to promote him captain—a promotion entirely justified by his conduct in the recent battle. It was to Bligh's first lieutenant that Admiral De Winter surrendered, and if anyone was to be promoted post-captain it should, to my mind, have been he. You will perhaps understand now why I nominated Grant for promotion. It was the only way of saving his career. I can't tell you how sorry I am that I could save him only at your expense.'

There was a long silence while Delancey stared unseeingly out of the stern windows as if fascinated to watch the water-hoy coming alongside the next ship in the line. Someone had thrown a rope and now she was secure. The other hoy would be laden with provisions. . . . . Was the scene real? Was it all true what the captain had been saying?

'. . . no reflection on you in any way,' Trollope's voice continued. 'It is my own belief that your promotion will follow and I need hardly say that I shall do my utmost for you. Lord Duncan knows the situation and thinks highly of you. His covering letter will accompany my recommendation, both written in the strongest terms.'

'Thank you, sir,' Delancey heard himself saying. 'Have you considered what your decision means to me?'

'I have indeed considered it and also discussed it with Lord Duncan. That you should be disappointed I entirely understand.'

'It is not a matter, sir, of disappointment. What you propose is to disgrace me in the eyes of the fleet. Sixteen ships of the line take part in a general engagement, one in which the enemy is not merely defeated but destroyed. Back at our fleet anchorage 15 out of 16 captains are thanked and decorated, one of them

posthumously, and one of them is court-martialled for cowardice. Fourteen out of 15 first lieutenants are promoted and one is
not, the promotion going to another officer who was not present
at the battle. Why is the one name omitted? Is it another
instance of cowardice or disaffection? What went wrong aboard
the *Russell?* Whatever it was cannot have been the captain's
fault, for he was singled out for the honour of knighthood. So
the first lieutenant was himself to blame for something about
which the others are sworn to silence. What a sad end to what
might have been a promising career!'

'Rubbish, Mr Delancey! Everyone knows that you did your
duty under fire.'

'Look, sir, I am not especially proud of my part in the recent
battle. War is war and we did what we had to do. We came
away without a man killed and only a handful wounded. The
battle over, I, for one, don't pose as a hero. But neither do I deserve the stigma of cowardice with which I am to be branded.'

'I never heard such nonsense, Delancey, and I think your attitude tells against you as an officer. Making every allowance
for your disappointment, I think you are making heavy weather
out of a faint headwind. I shall explain the situation to your
messmates and make it known to the other captains.
Remember that you are not missing promotion. You are in fact
to be promoted from acting first lieutenant to substantive first
lieutenant. And next time we go into action your promotion will
follow.'

'Leaving me junior, sir, to all the officers who are being promoted now.'

'Well, maybe. But remember that you may still be made post
ahead of them. It is very much a matter of luck, I grant you. I
have myself every confidence, however, that your early promotion is certain.'

'In the meanwhile, Sir Henry, there is only one course open
to me. I place my resignation in your hands, sir, and will con-

firm this in writing this afternoon.'

'Don't do anything so foolish, man. Sleep on it. Give yourself time to reflect. By to-morrow, depend on it, you will see things differently. I believe you started your naval career on the lower deck. To have risen from ordinary seaman to be first lieutenant of a 74-gun ship is quite an achievement. Did you originally expect to rise to that rank? And now you are ready to throw everything away at the very first setback. I beg you not to do anything so foolish.'

'I am willing and will think myself privileged to serve elsewhere, Sir Henry. I cannot, however, remain with the North Sea Fleet.'

'You are quite mistaken in your ideas and have gone a long way to convince me that I was right in my choice. You must believe, however, that I still think highly of you as an officer. In return for the wardroom's hospitality on a recent occasion I propose to ask all my officers to dine with me today. We shall be better supplied than usual and I have something out of the ordinary in the way of liquor. I shall make it clear on this occasion that I entirely approve of your conduct in the recent battle. I shall add that I need you as first lieutenant and that you have been good enough to refuse promotion at my special request. That will put an end to the possibility of any rumour circulating to your disadvantage.'

'Thank you, Sir Henry. I am deeply grateful for your consideration but must ask that you say nothing about my refusing promotion. I sincerely hope that your dinner party will be a great success, but I shall not be among those present. It is, I realise, practically unknown for an officer to decline his captain's invitation. On the present occasion I have no alternative. You shall have my resignation in writing, Sir Henry, together with my request for permission to go ashore. It is with real regret that I make my apologies. Your dinner should indeed be a memorable occasion. I am only sorry that I cannot be there.'

☆ ☆

The Fireship

DELANCEY was to realise in later years that he had behaved badly on this occasion and that he should have shown more consideration for Sir Henry Trollope and indeed for Alexander Grant. The story might have ended differently if Trollope had been more of a friend to Delancey, introducing him to the Trollope family and asking him to their town house. Delancey had all along been made to feel that he was a poor substitute for Grant and that he was not to be regarded as Trollope's follower in the service. He thought less, therefore, of ending what friendship there was. In fairness to Trollope it is clear that he still did what he could for Delancey, perhaps from a doubt in his mind as to the fairness of the decision he had made. Lord Duncan too must have added a word in Delancey's favour, a word which came from the hero of the hour. The result was that when Delancey called at the Admiralty a few days later he was told that he would be posted, as Lieutenant and Commander, to the fireship *Spitfire* on the Irish Station.

'A *fireship*?' he asked incredulously. 'I had forgotten that such vessels were still in commission.'

'There are fourteen, sir, to be exact,' said the clerk, adjusting his spectacles and running his finger down the list.

'What, fourteen in commission?'

'No, some are in ordinary.'

'But what are they supposed to do? I should suppose that

fireships were last used in the reign of Charles II.'

'Those we have were mostly built between 1781 and 1783, copied from the French sloop *Amazon* and intended, I believe, for use at the Siege of Gibraltar.'

'They never reached Gibraltar,' said Delancey, who had been there at the time.

'No,' the clerk admitted. 'They were built at the smaller outports—Shoreham, Sandgate, Wivenhoe—and were still being refitted and modified when the last war came to an end.'

'And the *Spitfire?*'

'Let's see now—hum—hum—Yes, built at Ipswich in 1782, ship-rigged, measuring 422 tons, 108 feet and ten inches long on the gun-deck, armed with fourteen 18-pounder carronades and established for a crew of fifty-five. Do you know the *Hazard*, sloop, of 24 guns? Well, *Spitfire* would be a sister ship to her but with double the quantity of gunpowder and less than half the number of men.'

'But used in what way?'

'Well, sir, here at the Admiralty that is hardly our concern. I have been told that fireships are often used to carry messages, fetch supplies, and make themselves generally useful in commerce protection.'

'Where is she now?'

'At Cork, to be sure.'

'And her last commander?'

'He resigned, sir, for reasons of health. And now, if you'll excuse me, sir, I have other work to do. If you would care to call again tomorrow forenoon—no, better the next day—you shall have your orders in writing and a warrant for the passage.'

Delancey left the Admiralty with mixed feelings. He had missed his promotion and was to be consoled with—a fireship. To be Master and Commander was to have the title of 'Captain' and see one's name on a list of Commanders, known candidates for post rank. A Lieutenant-Commander, to use the

more recent term, was still on the Lieutenants list and posted to
the command of a vessel too small to justify the appointment of
a Commander. His men would refer to him as 'Captain' but his
seniority in the Lieutenants list would be unchanged. He had
himself had the temporary command of a cutter on one occasion and knew that this was no road to further promotion. A
fireship was not quite the same thing but he had not realised
that such vessels still existed.

Thinking of the description he had been given, he realised
that the *Spitfire* would have men enough to work the ship but not
enough to fight an action except in self-defence against an
enemy corvette or privateer. Her carronades, with their smaller
gun-crews, would probably make it just possible to fight the one
broadside. But what role was a fireship supposed to play?
Delancey knew that Sir Francis Drake had used them against
the Spaniards but that was over two centuries ago. They had
not been used within the lifetime of anyone now in the service,
of that he felt almost certain. They might have been improvised
on occasion, he thought. A captured merchantman might
sometimes have been used, when set alight, to flush the enemy
out of an anchorage. He was not sure that he had heard of an
instance but he could imagine a situation in which such an
action might be justified. But the odds would be impossibly
great against a proper fireship, built for the purpose, being on
hand when wanted. And yet here was the *Spitfire*, built as recently as 1782!

His mind went back to Gibraltar and to his service there as a
midshipman. The allied fleet at Algeciras had certainly been
an ideal target for a fireship attack but then the enemy had
taken the obvious precautions, with a boom in position and
boats rowing guard. There would have had to be two attacks,
one to destroy the boom, the other to throw in the fireships.
There must have been some such plan under discussion at the
time, the *Spitfire* and her sister ships being the result. Each

would provide the ideal means of shelving a lieutenant who
was proving a nuisance.

Why does this have to happen to *me?*—this was Delancey's
first thought. But there went with it a deeper and more insistent
feeling of pleasant anticipation—illogical, absurd and yet
undeniably present. Delancey had commanded a ship before,
the privateer *Nemesis.* He had once commanded a revenue
cutter, the *Rose,* and before that (for a week or two) the cutter
Royalist. But the *Spitfire* would represent his first chance to command a regular man-of-war. He would be on his own and he
realised that this was what he liked. Fourteen of his contem-
poraries had been promoted, one even to post rank, but not all
of them would be given an immediate command. So far as that
went, he was lucky. But who could tell? There was a big element of luck in these things. A fireship, well handled, could destroy a ship of the line! The drawback was that she would
destroy herself in the act and leave her captain without a command. Or was there some established custom in such a case,
providing that he should be given the next vacancy?

While thus lost in thought Delancey was walking towards
Charing Cross. He presently became aware that he was over-
taking two other naval officers, walking more slowly still and
deep in argument over some question of seniority.

'But I'm positive that Jennings was with Hotham off Genoa
in '95, and I think was in command of the *Minerva.*'

'No, sir, he was not posted until the following year, which
makes him junior to Ridley.'

'Fiddlesticks! He is Ridley's senior by a year at the least and
there are not a dozen names between him and you.'

'Your memory deceives you, sir. Jennings has only the one
epaulette and won't hoist the other for another twelvemonth or
more. I don't know who commanded the *Minerva* in '95 but it
can't have been Jennings.'

'What do you wager, sir? I'll lay five guineas that he has his second epaulette.'

'Make it ten, sir? Your money, I warn you, is as good as lost.'

'Done, by God! Ten guineas it shall be!'

'And let's settle the matter now. Walk back with me to the Admiralty library and we'll decide the question by a glance at the printed list.'

'Very well, sir. You'll see I'm right!'

The two captains, one red faced and choleric, the other grey and obstinate, went about smartly and headed back towards the Admiralty, fairly brushing Delancey aside as they changed course. He for his part went slowly on towards the more economic lodging he had taken in St Martin's Lane. His previous lodging in Piccadilly had been more suitable for an officer of higher rank—of the rank, in fact, which he had hoped to attain.

The scrap of argument he had overheard had given him an idea. That the Admiralty building included a library was news to him but it seemed probable (now he heard of it) that such a book collection might include some work in which the fireship and its uses would be described. In his years of service he had heard nothing about fireships. He felt, therefore, that he should learn something about them before he left for Ireland. Their possibilities must have been discussed at the time that the *Spitfire* and her consorts had been laid down. Someone must have had grounds for believing in them and he must have been able to support his argument by some appeal to fairly recent experience. On what occasions had they been employed and with what result? When and how had they been used—and where, for that matter, and why?

The Admiralty library proved a disappointment. There were shelves of leather-bound volumes from floor to ceiling and even a ladder for reaching those which would otherwise have been out of reach. The librarian, however, was absent through illness and the youth who was his only assistant did no more than dust the volumes, professing to have no knowledge of their contents.

He came up, nevertheless, with a useful suggestion:

'There's a gentleman, sir, who might be able to advise you. Mr John Bruce is librarian to the East India Company. He has been here a great deal of late, preparing a report for Mr Secretary Dundas. You would have seen him had you come yesterday at this hour.'

Acting on this suggestion, Delancey made his way to Leadenhall Street and found Mr Bruce in a library which was larger and better furnished than that of the Admiralty. Bruce was a middle-aged Scotsman, historiographer (as he explained) to the Honourable East India Company, once a professor of logic but now librarian and archivist. He was very full of his current assignment, something to do with Conjunct Expeditions, but swore Delancey to secrecy before deciding that he should in fact be told nothing about it. He revealed no special interest in fireships but confessed to knowing something of their history.

'For this,' he explained, 'we must go back to the reign of that illustrious monarch, Queen Elizabeth, who faced foes as numerous and implacable as those now threatening our present sovereign. There is indeed a striking resemblance between these two reigns, the threat of Republican France being as dangerous today as was then the threat of Papist Spain and Portugal to which the Netherlands were then attached. For the ordinary gentleman it may be enough to consult the more popular works, the history written by Oliver Goldsmith or John Campbell's *Lives of the Admirals*—although the latter was published as long ago as 1742—but to discover the truth we need to go more deeply—'

'And what, if we did so, should we find about fireships?'

'Ah, yes . . . fireships. There can be no doubt that Sir Francis Drake was influenced by his knowledge of an earlier exploit in which a fireship, laden with explosives, was used with great effect. I refer, as you will no doubt have guessed, to—'

'But when, sir, were they *last* used?'

With great difficulty, Mr Bruce was persuaded to consider a later period in history.

'Well, they were used by the French against the Dutch in the Battle of Stromboli in 1676. Three of them were launched against De Ruyter's flagship but were driven off and destroyed. In the Battle off Palermo, on the other hand, which took place later in the same year, the Spanish flagship was attacked by fireships and blew up. Several other Spanish ships were destroyed in the same way by Tourville's fleet. Fireships were used by both sides at that period but the French had more of them—nine, I think—at Palermo.'

'But how were they used in the last war?'

'Let me see, now. They appeared, beyond question, in several of the engagements. Admiral Hughes had several with him in India. Use was made of them undoubtedly.'

'But when, sir, and how?'

'I can recollect no particular occasion. They had been used, of course, in the previous war.'

'Yes, sir?'

'The French used them in the defence of Quebec in 1759—without success. But those, I suspect, were merchantmen fitted up for the occasion. Ah, but I recall now one other incident, in the Mediterranean. I came across it while seeking information on a different subject—one that is secret, you will understand. Yes, I made a note in what I call my commonplace book. Here it is . . . There were five Spanish galleys at St Tropez in 1742, enemy ships in what was then a neutral port. They fired on the *Kingston* and Captain Richard Norris of that ship sent in the *Duke* fireship, commanded by a Mr Callis. So well did he carry out his orders that all five galleys were destroyed. I have noted, I see, that Callis was immediately posted to the *Assistance* of 50 guns.'

'He was promoted?' asked Delancey, hopefully.

'Yes, I think so. He had, I think, been only Master and Commander.'

'And you can recall no later instance of a fireship being used for the purpose for which she was built?'

'No, I think Captain Callis's exploit must have been the last occasion. At one stage in the compilation of a report for circulation in the Cabinet—its general purpose being of course secret—I thought that a use might be found for fireships at this present crisis in our history, bearing in mind the similarity between the present situation and that which confronted Queen Elizabeth. After making some notes—as for example on the Battle of Stromboli—I had to recognise that they no longer appear in battle. I remember now that this was the conclusion I reached. It was clear, on the other hand, that they were still being built and commissioned, I suppose for general use.'

'Thank you, sir, for this valuable information. I must take no more of your time, understanding as I do that you have important work on hand.'

'And I must rely on you, sir, to divulge nothing of what I have told you. Secrecy is vital to the work upon which I am engaged.'

Delancey gave his word on this point, taking his leave in the certainty that he could not reveal what he had never been told. What he still failed to understand—and was never destined to discover—was why a type of vessel should still be built in 1782, and commissioned in 1797, which had last been of service in 1742.

Dining that day at a Coffee House in the Strand, Delancey made mental note of two facts that had so far emerged from his studies. First of all, it was evident to him that a fireship would never operate on her own. There must always be at least one other ship in company, commanded by an officer to whom the fireship's commander would be junior. There were two reasons for this: first, a fireship was too vulnerable to capture by a ship of her own size or smaller; and, second, there must be another ship to which her boats could row after the unmanned fireship had been set on a course. The other fact to emerge by inference was that a fireship's target must be at anchor, preferably, and should ideally be a group of vessels rather than a single ship. Captain Callis clearly owed his promotion to the fact that the French galleys were moored close together, making a wide target, and were under the illusion of safety in a neutral port. According to Norris the galleys had fired first (a likely story!) and it was he, of course, who ordered the attack. Had there been a single galley the fireship would probably have missed it. But, apart from that, the attack would not have been made, the fireship to be sacrificed being as valuable as the enemy vessel to be destroyed. It would have been a case of a pawn lost on either side and no advantage gained. But what about Palermo? He guessed that the flagship there had been dismasted and left as a sitting target. The chances of a fireship hitting a moving enemy must be remote. Her chance of hitting a single victim at anchor would depend, above all, on her captain's determination. He would at some stage have to abandon ship but the later the better. The longer the distance to be covered with the wheel lashed the more chance there was of the ship going off course, especially while under fire. The need was for a cool head to direct and a brave man to make the attack.

Delancey collected his letter of appointment on the following day, together with a passage warrant, and set off that evening in the mail coach for Bristol. The point of departure was the Post Office at St Martin-le-Grand and the coach left at eight in the evening as the church bells struck.

'To the minute, as usual!' said Delancey's neighbour, watch in hand, 'and we'll be in Bath to the minute as I'm willing to wager!'

'Even on a cold December night?' asked Delancey, to humour him.

'No doubt of it, sir!' said the old tradesman, evidently on his hobby horse. 'The ice on the road is nothing to Jack Salter who is driving us.'

The truth of this was evident from the way London was left behind in what seemed a matter of minutes. The coaching enthusiast introduced himself as Laurence Bagshaw, draper, of Cheapside.

'Did you ever hear, sir, of John Palmer of Bristol?'

'No, Mr Bagshaw,' replied Delancey, I don't know that I did.'

'Well, so far as the mail coaches go we owe everything to him.'

'Is that so? Was he Postmaster-General, then?'

'No, sir. He was manager of the Orchard Street Theatre in Bath, now the Royal. Mrs Siddons was the great actress of his time—nay, she's acting still, come to think of it—and she often had to appear in the same week at Drury Lane, at Bath and at Bristol. The problem was to save her from excessive fatigue. It was John Palmer who persuaded Mr Pitt that the royal mails should go by coach, making a daily service, run like clockwork and as safe as the Bank.'

'How were the mails carried before, then?'

'Why, by a postboy on horseback! All that's left of him, sir, is the horn.'

On this improved system the Royal Mail coach was in Bristol next morning by 9 o'clock and Delancey had already learnt in Bath that the packet for Cork would not sail until the following day.

To him the most important thing about Bristol was that it was the town where his sister Rachel lived. She had been brought up, as he had been, in St Peter Port but had married John Sedley in 1776 and was now a respected wife and mother. She was no great correspondent, however, and the letters he had received from her over the last twenty years had been infrequent and brief. She had several children, this much he knew, and her husband had formerly been a strong supporter of Mr Edmund Burke, for many years one of Bristol's Members of Parliament.

On this, his first visit to Bristol, Delancey had no difficulty in finding where Rachel lived. 'Alderman Sedley? Why, he lives off Queen's Square, right in the town centre.' He gathered from his inquiries that Sedley was a West India merchant of some note, with some interest in sugar refining and in the manufacture of sailcloth. The Sedleys' house, when he found it, was solid and respectable, the door being opened by a negro servant.

'Richard!' cried Rachel, hugging a brother she had not seen for so long but whom she did not fail to recognise.

They exchanged news, she being able to boast of four children, the eldest son already established as an attorney, the youngest daughter just out of school. Then John Sedley came in, looking portly, prosperous and aldermanic and Richard Delancey had to describe his career all over again. He dined with the family and heard all the news of Bristol.

'And in what trade, would you suppose,' asked John 'do we employ the largest number of our ships?'

'The American trade?' asked Delancey.

'No, sir. The trade with Ireland! They are not, of course, our largest vessels but they number over a hundred. The Irish trade is perhaps our oldest, shared with Liverpool, and you will realise the anxiety we feel about the present situation in Ireland. We hear of nothing but sedition and what will be the result if the French actually land? You may picture the concern we felt when we heard of the mutiny and realised that there was nothing to prevent the French invading Ireland. They don't seem to have realised their opportunity until it had nearly passed. Then came the news of Lord Duncan's victory and we thought that the worst danger must be over. What do you think, Richard? Is Ireland still open to attack?'

'It is still open to a raid, to a landing of troops from a small squadron. I don't think that a whole fleet of transports could be collected without our knowledge. Nor could it sail, I think, without being intercepted.'

'That's my opinion too, Richard. But I have close connections, you will understand, with Cork and hear regularly from my friends who are established there. Of one thing they are certain and that is the activity of French agents in every part of Ireland. Some of the rumours they hear are false—of that I am well assured—but they are well informed and sensible men and they know for certain that there are spies in every seaport and that their activity is increasing. If we accept that fact we must suppose that it is the prelude to some actual landing.'

'I am very ready to believe that some such operation is being planned. I can only add that I shall do my best to prevent it succeeding, and that officers senior to me will be still better placed to frustrate whatever scheme is finally adopted. Our cruisers will not be idle, I can assure you.'

That evening John Sedley saw to it that Richard should meet several other merchants. They were all concerned about Ireland, all convinced that French efforts in that direction were being intensified. Delancey was prepared to believe them and asked for introduction to their partners in Cork, the men from whom these reports derived. From various merchants he finally collected eight letters of introduction; three of them, however, to the same man, Mr Jeremiah Coyne, provision merchant of Cork and Waterford. It would seem that he was either more alert than others or more committed to the English interest—or merely perhaps more apprehensive.

When the time came to say goodbye next morning, after a night spent at the Sedleys, Richard was able to congratulate Rachel on the success of her marriage, as also on her promising family, and thank John for his hospitality, as also for opening up what might be a useful source of intelligence. John's carriage took him to the quayside and he was soon on board the packet for Cork.

Passing the ships moored in the Kingroad and seeing the vessels under sail in the Bristol Channel, he could see how important Bristol must be. He could also appreciate that Ireland was vital to the trade on which Bristol and Liverpool depended. The smart West Indiamen he could see might be bound for Jamaica and would return with sugar but they would actually call at an Irish port on the outward passage. It was from Ireland they obtained their provisions and at least some of their crew. It was often in an Irish anchorage that the convoy would assemble. With the French in Ireland, following a successful revolt, the continuance of this trade would be difficult, perhaps impossible. All this the French must know. For them to intrigue with the Irish rebels was as natural as for the British to intrigue with the French royalists. Head of the British system of naval intelligence was Captain Philip d'Auvergne, Prince of Bouillon, for whom he himself had once undertaken a dangerous mission. Who, he wondered, was Philip d'Auvergne's opponent in Ireland, the secret agent whose work would prepare for the next landing of French troops? There would be a British fleet within striking distance of Brest. There would be British cruisers off all the French Atlantic ports. There were British cruisers on the Irish coast and he was to command one of them. But the identification of that one secret agent could be more important than the combined efforts of every ship involved. He wondered who might have been given the task of hunting down this enemy. Would his identity be known to the senior naval officer at Cork?

'Good morning, Mr Delancey.' It was Mr Bagshaw who had come to join him on the lee side of the packet's quarterdeck. 'A brisk morning, sir, with a chilly wind. What a sight it is to see all these ships under sail! How many millions have been invested in the foreign trade ships alone, ignoring the coasters! It makes you think, sir—makes you think!'

Delancey agreed that the spectacle was one to give pause for thought. 'There is much at stake,' he admitted, 'and Ireland is the key to the situation.'

'Interesting to hear you say that,' said Bagshaw; 'we who are engaged in the drapery trade would agree with you. Were Ireland to go, Britain would be lost. But the French are not having it all their own way, nor the Dutch neither!'

Bagshaw sat next to Delancey at dinner in the cabin and professed a knowledge of Cork going back over the last decade. Yes, he had known Mr Coyne for years; a man much concerned with the victualling of ships. Oh, yes, the French agents were active—the fact was well known—but the Irish rebels were very apt to betray each other. A man like Jeremiah Coyne could be trusted, he had a solid interest in the provision trade, but it was a question whom you could trust—for, after all, they could never trust each other! Sharing a bottle of wine with Mr Bagshaw, Delancey came to know more about the climate of opinion in southern Ireland.

On a cold and frosty morning the packet came into Cork harbour where several men-of-war were at anchor. Delancey looked with interest at the grey, bleak town and the hills beyond which had recently had a sprinkling of snow. The quaysides looked busy and there were many oared boats on the water. There was a gleam of sunshine through a tattered canopy of cloud and one man-of-war was momentarily lit up palely against the sombre background. It was the *Spitfire* beyond question and Delancey knew her from the description he had been given. A sister ship to the *Hazard*—yes, that was the one, no doubt of it. He was presently rowed ashore and saw that there was an elderly lieutenant on the quayside. As soon as he landed this officer came up to him, saluted, and introduced himself as William Partridge.

'I'm first lieutenant of the *Spitfire*, sir, and the only other commissioned officer. You can see her on the far side of the anchorage. I heard tell that you was to be expected, sir, and have a boat at the other end of the quay.'

'Thank you, Mr Partridge.'

'The senior naval officer at Cork is Captain Ashley of the *Seahorse* frigate of 38 guns. Should you wish to pay your respects to Captain Ashley, the boat can take you directly to the frigate.'

'Thank you, Mr Partridge. I shall first take command of the *Spitfire*. Send two men here for my gear. I shall go aboard at once and on to the *Seahorse* afterwards.'

'Aye, aye, sir.' The elderly Mr Partridge ambled off to where the *Spitfire*'s boat could be seen at the harbour steps.

Delancey felt that he had been needlessly brusque but Partridge, a promoted gunner or boatswain, was aged about fifty to judge from his looks, and it was essential to leave no doubt as to who was in command. There was in fact, as he soon discovered, no trouble to be anticipated from Partridge, whose ambitions had been rather exceeded, if anything, by his present appointment and whose relief at being superseded was almost pathetic.

'I'm more than glad to see you, sir. It has been rather a strain on me since our last captain went ashore. We are not as well manned as I should like to see. The fact is, sir—and I feel bound to tell you this, sir, at the outset—some of our crew were drafted from the *Montagu* and some from the *Sandwich* . . .'

'The *Sandwich*?'

'Yes, sir. It was thought proper to split up the crews which were foremost in the mutiny. About fifteen in all were sent to the *Spitfire*. They regard service in a fireship as a kind of punishment, thinking that the ship is likely to blow up.'

'But that is nonsense. Any man-of-war carries enough gunpowder to ensure her own destruction were fire to reach the magazine. A fireship may carry a greater quantity but her crew run no more risk than they would in any other ship. They might be blown higher but they can't be killed twice.'

'So they've been told, sir, but I have little confidence in the crew we have. There are two good master's mates, a very good gunner, a useful midshipman and all too little else.'

Within half an hour Delancey was on the deck of the *Spitfire*, the boatswain having piped the side, and was looking about him. The ship, as he had seen from the approaching boat, was in very fair order, neither better nor worse than the average. The general effect was workmanlike rather than artistic. The men seemed a mixed lot with attitudes varying from the careless to the sullen. Standing at the break of the quarterdeck, backed by Partridge, the boatswain and gunner, Delancey read his commission audibly and swiftly and then dismissed the crew. It was too cold to keep the men on deck and he postponed his inspection of the ship until the following day. While the gig was being brought to the main entry he asked only two questions:

'I see that we don't have the grapnels rigged.'

'No, sir,' replied Partridge. 'We can rig them in four minutes.'

'Are there boats for the entire crew?'

'Yes, sir. We have one more than a sloop of the same tonnage would carry.'

'Thank you, Mr Partridge. I am going on board the *Seahorse* but expect to return shortly. I shall then want to see the ship's papers—log, letter-books, ledgers and accounts.'

As the boat pushed off, the boatswain piping the side, Delancey, looking critically at the ship's paintwork, noticed that the gun-ports were hinged at the bottom instead of the top. This, he realised, must be a fireship characteristic. But why? Thinking it over, he realised that the flames, when the ship was alight, might burn the ropes which opened the gun-ports. The ports would then close, reducing the through-draught between decks and blocking the gun muzzles. The preferred plan was that the rising heat would fire the guns during the approach to the target, discouraging such enemy boats as might be sent to deflect the fireship from her course. Ports hinged at the bottom would tend to come open if closed and stay open if already agape.

As for the grapnels, he knew that these were attached by chain to a fireship's yardarms and bowsprit with the idea of locking her with the target ship. To have them rigged in advance would be a mistake—he could see that now—because the fireship could then be identified as such, known to be undermanned and vulnerable and yet recognised as a possible danger. In certain rather unlikely circumstances a fireship could be the ace in the pack but her effectiveness must dwindle from the moment the threat was apparent. Up till the last moment the fireship must look like any other sloop.

Delancey was still considering these points as his boat came alongside the *Seahorse*. A few minutes later he was reporting to Captain Ashley, who turned out to be intelligent, well-informed, capable and pleasant. The interview was brief and formal, ending, however, with an invitation to dinner that day.

'Besides my first lieutenant, Mr Goodrich, my other guest will be Captain Kerr of the *Vulture*, the eldest son of Lord Lichfield.'

Delancey accepted the invitation with pleasure and returned to the *Seahorse* that afternoon. It was not, as he guessed, to be a merely social occasion. One object of the dinner party on board the *Seahorse* was evidently to introduce Delancey to Captain Kerr on a convivial occasion. He knew from Partridge that the *Spitfire* had recently been at sea in company with the *Vulture* and he assumed that Ashley's intention was to place the fireship again under Kerr's orders, arranging that the two commanders should become acquainted beforehand.

This part of the scheme was a failure, Kerr seeming to dislike Delancey from the outset. Aged about twenty-four, Kerr was handsome, tall, white-faced, fair-haired and patronising. As heir to a vast estate he added self-importance to a fair measure of natural ability. He indicated in all but words that he was accustomed to the society of gentlemen and had little use for upstart officers from the Channel Islands.

'Forgive my ignorance, captain,' he drawled, 'but I failed to catch the name of your last ship.'

'I served in the *Russell*, sir, of 74 guns, commanded by Sir Henry Trollope.'

'Ah, yes, I remember now; and before that in the *Glatton* . . . and I take it that you were Trollope's first lieutenant?'

'Yes, sir.'

'And I am right, am I not, in assuming that you played some part in the Battle of Camperdown?'

'Yes, sir.'

'But I remember being told that all first lieutenants had been promoted after Camperdown. Why are you the exception, I wonder, still on the lieutenants' list? You would seem to have been unfortunate, eh?'

Captain Ashley intervened at this point:

'I know all the circumstances, Captain Kerr, and they are greatly to Mr Delancey's credit.'

'Ah, but of *course*, sir! I showed no more than idle interest. I am told, moreover, Captain Delancey, that you once commanded a privateer. What an interesting career you would seem to have had!'

'Interesting perhaps but unaided by interest.'

'You are at one there with the good Mr Partridge—a very worthy man, I always think.'

Captain Ashley intervened again.

'No officer can have too wide or varied an experience. But Mr Delancey has not yet served in Ireland and there is some general information he needs to know. Pass the wine, Mr Goodrich, and be ready, Captain Kerr, to add any significant fact that escapes me. In general, I believe in the rule against discussing service matters at table but I feel entitled to describe for you the general situation. You will recall, no doubt, the attempt of the French to invade Ireland in December of last year. Vice-Admiral Morard de Galles attempted a landing in Bantry Bay, the troops to be led by General Hoche. The attempt failed in bad weather—'

'No thanks to Lord Bridport,' Kerr added.

'But we have every reason to think that some further effort will be made this next summer. The French will have learnt at least that winter is not the best time and they may well have concluded that Bantry is not the best place. Much of Ireland is disaffected and we hear that French agents are active. There are troops here under Lord Lake and there are loyal regiments of militia but the situation is tempting from the French point of view. We do not suppose that the French have a large army to spare but it would be greatly to their interest to supply the Irish rebels with arms, ammunition, direction and encouragement. The landing of even a small French force would be a disaster. My task, therefore, is to patrol the Irish coast and give early warning of any such attempt. For this purpose the ships I have, frigates and sloops, are quite sufficient. I lack the force to defeat the enemy but have enough to observe and report. I may add that a fireship may do this work as well as a sloop, which is why the *Spitfire* has been added to my squadron. I am responsible for the coast from here round the west coast to Malinmore Head in Donegal and my present inclination is to keep an especially close watch on the shores of Connaught.'

'May I ask why, sir?' said Delancey, thinking that the question was expected.

'For this reason,' replied Ashley, 'that the French relied last time on a south-westerly gale. The gale that favoured their passage from Brest was enough to keep Lord Bridport at Spithead. So far so good, but the same gale blew straight into Bantry Bay and every other bay from Dingle to Baltimore— they all face south-west—making a landing all but impossible.

They will have realised by now that there is better shelter between Galway and Donegal.'

'And may I ask, sir, whether our intelligence reports point to the same conclusion?' asked Kerr as one who already knew the answer.

'I cannot claim that they do. We hear of sedition and subversion in almost every part of the country.'

'So the French might equally land on the east coast north of Wexford?'

'Very true, Captain Kerr, but that is outside the limits of my station.'

Delancey gained a clear idea that afternoon of what the Cork squadron had to do and learnt at the same time to respect the abilities of Captain Ashley. What irritated him was the atmosphere created by the aristocratic Captain Kerr, who showed no more than a formal respect for his senior officer and did all he could to humiliate those junior to him. Kerr was neither fool nor coward—so much Delancey knew from gossip—but he seemed to have the utmost contempt for his social inferiors. He made it apparent that Delancey was, in his opinion, quite unequal to the command of any man-of-war, even the obsolete absurdity to which he had been posted. He sneered at the ill-named *Spitfire*, threw doubt on Delancey's seamanship and courage and wondered all but audibly how some men, unnamed, should have reached commissioned rank at all. Ashley's patience and courtesy made a complete contrast but could not be enough in itself to make the dinner party a success.

The squadron remained in port over Christmas, as might be expected, and this gave Delancey his opportunity to call on certain of the local merchants, beginning with Mr Jeremiah Coyne, who turned out to be a youngish man of evident ability. Confirming all he had written to his friends in Bristol, he was sure that the French system of intelligence was highly organised. It was not a haphazard affair, he emphasised, with odd dissidents sending random information to France. There were, rather, trained agents working under the direction of a central headquarters and bound together by a common purpose.

'At the centre of the network is a character known to his numbered subordinates as Fabius. He is believed to be constantly on the move but working from a base which may well be the point chosen for the landing.'

There would certainly be at least one enemy agent in Cork, Mr Coyne added, but he did not profess to know who he was. After gaining rather similar information from two other Cork business men, Delancey reported this gossip to Captain Ashley.

'You have acted very properly in telling me what you have heard. I think myself that Coyne's information is probably correct and indeed I have heard the same story before. You should realise, however, that we too have our agents. They are not my direct concern but I know of their existence and have the means of communicating with them through an intermediary.'

'So I should be wrong, sir, to seek intelligence on my own?'

'I would say, rather, that you should listen to all the information you are offered but that you should not play at being a secret agent, and that for two reasons. In the first place, you cannot be secret while in uniform. In the second place, our agents might not welcome your assistance or mine. We do best, in general, to stick to our own trade.'

Delancey had to realise that Captain Ashley was right. He hoped, nevertheless, that the agents on the British side were active. To patrol the whole Irish coast was no easy task. It would be much simplified if the probable French landing place were known in advance. It should become apparent from previous rebel activity in the area. Or was the elusive Mr Fabius too clever for that?

The day after this interview (January 3rd, 1798) was that on which the *Vulture* and *Spitfire* had been ordered to sail. As the hour had been fixed beforehand the *Vulture*'s gun, soon after daylight, was needless and so, strictly speaking, was the signal to make sail. Delancey had his men ready, the cable hove short and the anchor ready to trip. Partridge was on the forecastle, ready to cat and fish the anchor. There was a fresh breeze blowing directly out of the harbour and Delancey acknowledged the signal, ordering Partridge to heave the anchor up. As soon as it had broken ground he gave his next orders through the speaking trumpet.

'Hoist the jib!' and then, 'Hoist the spanker!' With his small crew he thought it better to keep her under this reduced sail until the anchor had been cat-headed and fished.

From the *Vulture* came the boom of a second gun and the interrogative signal, 'Why did you not obey my order?'

'Acknowledge!' snapped Delancey and then shouted, 'Let fall the topsails!'

The *Vulture* was already under plain sail and gaining distance. 'Let fall the fore-course! Sheet home!'

Cursing inwardly, Delancey then made the signal for inability. He realised what he had already guessed, that Captain the Hon. Vincent Kerr was not an easy man with whom to work. He was to discover in the course of the next few months that this was a mild way of putting it. Kerr had a gift for self assertion and sarcasm. Delancey began to see the resignation of his predecessor in a different light.

☆ ☆

Fabius

IN THOSE EARLY DAYS in the *Spitfire*, sailing up the west coast of Ireland, caustic signals from Kerr were only part of the trouble. Bad weather was of course to be expected but, apart from that, Kerr had a habit of entering and quitting each inlet without so much as dropping anchor. In one way he thus made a useful impression on the Irish, suggesting that the Navy was everywhere and liable to appear in the most remote harbour without the slightest warning. There was no rest for the ships' crews, however, and hardly a chance to set foot ashore. It was during February and March that Delancey covered the whole of Kerr's cruising ground, knowing that his familiarity with the coastline would be of immense value if the French were to land. The two ships worked their way up the coasts of Galway and Donegal, circling Arannore and Tory Islands, entering such inlets as Sheep Haven and Mulroy Bay.

Things began then to improve and so in time did the weather. The *Spitfire* became a smarter ship with sail drill on which Captain Kerr was gradually ceasing to comment. Working their way north for the second time, the two ships called at Westport, at Broad Haven, and finally at Killala. Their stay there might have been as brief as Kerr's restless temper made usually inevitable but he and Delancey received an unusually pressing invitation from the protestant Bishop of Killala, whose official residence was at the Castle. The letter was no more than a friendly invitation to dinner but worded with a touch of urgency which Kerr could not ignore. There was clearly something on the Bishop's mind, some idea which he did not want to express in writing.

Both officers came ashore in the *Vulture*'s boat and a carriage and pair was waiting to take them from the landing place to the episcopal palace. Dr Stock himself met them at the front door. He was a portly and red-faced man of middle age, with no great appearance of learning or piety but looking decidedly worried.

'Captain Kerr! Captain Delancey! How very good of you to come. This way, gentlemen . . .' A manservant took their hats and the bishop led them into the drawing room where they were presented to Mrs Stock and to several daughters. Then the chaplain, Mr Ludlow, was introduced to them and reference made to several sons who were lurking uncertainly in the background. Dinner was announced soon afterwards and was served by well-intentioned but clumsy Irish maids. There were sounds of altercation in the kitchen and on one occasion the noise of broken crockery. Mrs Stock winced but ignored the disaster, talking rather loudly about social life in County Mayo and how different it was from that of her own home near Tunbridge Wells. The coastal scenery was beautiful, she confessed, but she and her husband greatly looked forward to their winter stay in Dublin.

'And is there a big protestant population round Killala, my lord?' asked Delancey.

'Alas, no,' said the bishop, 'there are the gentry of course, and some of their servants, the customs officers and a very few tradesmen, but the country folk are all catholic and have little or no education, I do what good I can but it is difficult to avoid a sense of isolation.'

'I trust, however,' said Delancey, 'that your lordship finds it peaceful here? There are parts of Ireland, I gather, where the peasants are in a state of actual rebellion.'

'So far we have been fortunate, sir, in that respect. I pray that we may be spared the troubles which afflict some other counties.'

What conversation there was depended mainly on the Bishop and Delancey, Mrs Stock saying little and her children, nothing. Captain Kerr was at his worst, barely civil and showing little respect for his host and hostess. He knew of no gentleman called Stock and concluded that nobody of consequence would be sent to so remote a diocese. One owed some show of politeness to a Bishop of Winchester or Salisbury but whoever heard of a Bishop of Killala? He rejected several of the dishes and left his wine almost untasted, doubting on principle whether a Dr Stock could have anything drinkable in his cellar. Delancey did his best but was frankly relieved when Mrs Stock and her children left the dining room, leaving the bishop to offer his guests a glass of port. Mr Ludlow had so far been silent but he was active now in placing the decanters on the table, as also in recommending the madeira, which Delancey found excellent.

'You may have wondered, gentlemen, why I was so urgent to have your company today. It is always pleasant to have visitors in a place as remote as this and sea officers are especially welcome at any time. I must be frank, however, and confess that I need your help. Mr Ludlow and I have noticed of late some activities in this neighbourhood which seem to us unusual. After six years in a diocese one has a clear idea of what one must expect. There are well-known characters whose haunts and whose sayings one has come to know. There are groups whose membership is unvarying, friendships which are long established and—I regret to add—hostilities which have become traditional. Last year we began to notice some inexplicable changes. This year the changes have been more marked. Taken severally no single event can be thought significant. Taken together, they create a disturbing situation.'

'What his lordship means,' said Mr Ludlow, 'is that folk whose manners were candid have become furtive; eager conversations have died away when we have entered a room. There have been strangers around whose presence has been unexplained and men have been absent without a word of their going or their return. We gain the impression that something is being planned, that some important event is expected.'

'Mr Ludlow puts it very well,' said the Bishop. 'You will understand that my position in Killala is not that of an English prelate in England. I am a priest, it is true, and am here to preach the gospel and explain the doctrines of the Church of England. There is also a sense in which I am a government official and am certainly regarded as such. If there is sedition I cannot stand idly by. If there is crime I must do what I can to prevent the criminal's escape from justice. I am not myself a justice of the peace but some of my clergy sit on the bench with my approval. Whether I like it or not I am part of Ireland's administration and in that capacity I am frankly alarmed.'

'You describe, my lord,' said Captain Kerr, 'a change in atmosphere. Is there any one single event or circumstance which I could report as a fact to my superior officer?'

'Yes, sir,' said Mr Ludlow, 'it is a fact that we have seen four catholic priests, strangers to this vicinity, within the last three weeks.'

'But is that so remarkable? This is a catholic country and priests are, surely, numerous?'

'Priests may be numerous,' said the Bishop, 'but they do not wander round each other's parishes. It is a question whether the men we have seen in clerical garb are priests at all.'

'Clerical costume makes a good disguise,' observed Mr Ludlow. 'No questions are asked—save by other clergy like his lordship—and you yourself, captain, see nothing odd in priests who come and go.'

'Would you think it odd, sir,' asked Kerr, 'if it were strange protestant clergy who behaved in this fashion?'

'Strange, sir?' Ludlow exclaimed, 'It would be all but impossible. The clergy of our church are few and are all known to us.'

'Very well then,' Kerr replied, 'I shall write a report containing the gist of your views on this matter, my lord. You will realise, however, that my wording must be rather vague. There will be similar reports from other areas, the general conclusion being that the peasants are restless. I beg leave to doubt, my lord, whether that will come as a surprise to the folk at Dublin Castle.'

'The point, sir,' said Mr Ludlow with vigour, 'is not that people are restless but that some mischief is brewing in one particular district.'

'What could French agents achieve, sir, supposing that these visiting priests are working for the enemy?'

'They could undermine the loyalty of the militia,' said Mr Ludlow promptly, 'and that, I suspect, is what they are doing.'

'You will understand, gentlemen,' said the bishop, 'that we have given some thought to this matter. We have said enough, though, and will leave you to draw your own conclusions. Let us turn to pleasanter subjects. Have you done any sea-fishing in this bay? If you are interested, my sons could show you where fish are to be caught. They have grown up here and are seldom ashore! They make their own crab-pots too . . .'

Rejoining the ladies, Captain Kerr made some slight effort at conversation with the daughters and Delancey talked about fishing with one of the boys. Then the carriage took them back to the landing place, where a boat was waiting from either ship. Before they parted, Delancey asked Kerr in private whether he was impressed by what the bishop had said about local unrest.

'No,' Kerr replied. 'The same, I suspect, could be said of any other place. I shall make a routine report and leave Captain Ashley to take what action he thinks appropriate. We shall sail with the morning's tide.'

'Aye, aye, sir,' said Delancey and stepped into his gig.

He wondered, as he approached the *Spitfire*, why Kerr had to make himself so unpleasant to people he met for the first time. There were odd moments when he almost liked Kerr, catching some hint of a character seldom revealed, but there was no denying that he had been needlessly brusque with the bishop. It seemed to him, on reflection, that the warning Kerr had been given came more from the chaplain than the bishop. There was a hint of the fanatic about Ludlow. He really hated popery, being a man from Londonderry, a puritan by descent, connection and choice. He was also, for that matter, a man of some intelligence, loyal to the crown and utterly opposed to any sort of revolution. The bishop was a good man in his way, perhaps genuinely religious and certainly a kind host but not a dominant personality. Left to himself, Delancey would have made a longer stay at Killala and made some inquiries on his own.

Later that day Delancey was told that a boat from the shore was alongside and that its young oarsman wished to see him. It was David Stock, the bishop's youngest son, and he brought a letter from Mr Ludlow, which read as follows:

Dear Captain Delancey,

Soon after your leaving us we have had an unexpected visitor, a clergyman called Matthew Clarke. I do not know what to make of him and the bishop would be more than grateful if you would come ashore again and give us the benefit of your advice. I would suggest that you wear civilian clothes and conceal your true profession and rank, professing to be a friend of the bishop who has come to advise him about repairing the castle.

I have the honour to be, sir,
Your humble servant,
William Ludlow

Delancey turned from this missive to its bearer, an active boy aged about twelve.

'Tell me, David, do you know what this letter is about?'

'Yes, sir.'

'You have seen this visitor, Mr Clarke?'

'Oh, yes, sir.'

'What do you think of him?'

'I don't quite know, sir.'

'Why is Mr Ludlow inclined to suspect him?'

'He can't understand why this man is here.'

'Very well then. Will you take me ashore in your boat?'

'Oh, yes, sir.'

Ten minutes later Delancey was on his way back to the landing place, sole passenger in a crazy and leaking patched-up rowing boat. The boat was old and battered but her proud owner knew the local waters as well as any fisherman, talking easily of where the tidal current set and of rocks which were wrongly shown on the chart. As Delancey soon discovered, young David did not talk readily about anything else.

There was no carriage this time at the landing place but David, having secured the boat, led Delancey to the castle by the shortest footpath. He was once more admitted but this time under the name of Mr Cartwright. Playing his part surprisingly well, the bishop thanked him for coming all the way from Belfast.

'You may think I am showing needless alarm, and I hope indeed that I am. My belief is, however, that early attention to any weakness in a building is a true economy. In England one suspects, sometimes, that a builder will make work for himself but here it is just the contrary. My local builder, Shamus O'Toole, will say, 'T''is foine, y'honour, the way it is,' just to save himself the trouble. Now you must meet my other guest, Mr Clarke, from Oxford. Mr Clarke, I want you to meet Mr Cartwright, an old friend of mine from Belfast.'

'Your servant, sir,' said Mr Clarke, and Delancey found himself looking at a plump, white-faced, middle-aged clergyman wearing spectacles and smiling benevolently on the world in general. He looked comfortable and prosperous, his black clothes being new, his cravat beautifully laundered.

'Welcome to Ireland, sir,' said Delancey. 'May I ask what brings you to these parts?'

'Mere curiosity, Mr Cartwright. I am fellow of an Oxford college but the suggestion was recently made to me that I should accept a living in Ireland; somewhere, I think, in Donegal. Before I decided one way or the other I thought I should see something of the country—or at least the less disturbed parts of it. His lordship, I need hardly say, has been kindness itself, and I recognise another Oxford man in Mr Ludlow here.'

It was arranged that both Clarke and Cartwright should stay for supper and both were taken to view the part of the castle about which the bishop professed to be anxious. 'It seems to me,' he explained, 'that the wall is tilting outwards with the thrust of the rafters and that a buttress is needed or perhaps even two.'

'Rafters do not ordinarily thrust, my lord,' said Delancey, remembering what little he knew of building construction, 'What thrust there is should be taken by the tie-beam. Perhaps I could look at the roof to-morrow when the light is better?'

Over supper Mr Clarke was much at his ease. He touched on the classics, mentioned a recent book of theology and deplored a recent election to a readership in the divinity school at Oxford. Mrs Stock, who had never been to Oxford, asked about social life there. Mr Clarke replied that ladies there were all too few, more was the pity. He hesitated for a moment when asked about the governing body of Oriel, the college at which he claimed to be fellow and tutor.

'I should perhaps have explained,' he said, 'that I have only just been elected, having been scholar of another college and subsequently chaplain to a nobleman in the north of England.'

Of which college had he formerly been a scholar? He named Merton and went on to talk of a sermon he had to deliver at the university church. Mr Ludlow listened patiently and then asked, innocently, 'You were a scholar of Merton, not a postmaster?'

Clarke appeared to ignore this question, and at that moment the bishop, a Cambridge man who had nothing to contribute on this topic was glad to talk instead about Donegal, the part of Ireland to which Mr Clarke was travelling. 'Good for sea trout,' he concluded, 'but a little remote.'

After supper the ladies withdrew for a while and Ludlow made an excuse to take Delancey aside, showing him a plan of the castle, and said quietly, 'This fellow was *not* at Merton. You talk to him while I tell the bishop.' Some more general talk followed over the dining table and then the bishop returned to the room with his chaplain.

'Ah, Mr Clarke,' he said rather solemnly, 'I have just been reminded that our most active magistrate here, Mr Galway of Crofton Park, near Ballina, is also a former student of Merton and might easily have been your contemporary there. He is due to visit Killala at noon tomorrow and would, I know, be glad to meet you and would be disappointed indeed to find you gone. I hope you can delay your departure for another day? And should you find your present lodging a trifle comfortless, I shall be more than willing to have you here as my guest.'

'Really, my lord,' replied Clarke, 'you overwhelm me with kindness. I must not, however, trespass any further on your hospitality. It so happens that I am expected at Sligo by tomorrow evening. I shall return to Ballina and will then have the honour of waiting on Mr Galway. While I do not remember meeting him, the name does sound familiar, I must confess.'

'That is not surprising,' said the Bishop, 'for he is cousin, I understand, to Dr Latimer, the present master of Oriel.'

'It is no doubt in that connection that I have heard of him, then. And now, my lord, I shall, with permission, take my leave, remembering that I have far to travel tomorrow.'

'Wait a little, Mr Clarke. I think you *should* meet Mr Galway tomorrow. You must understand that the country is disturbed, that a French landing is not impossible and that we look on strangers here with some suspicion. We see them as enemy agents planning rebellion against the lawful government. I must suppose that you can establish your innocence but I should warn you, sir, that you are presently suspect and liable to arrest.'

'You think, my lord, that I am a secret agent?'

'I would rather say that your account of yourself is not wholly convincing.'

'Did it occur to your lordship that I might be a secret agent but on the British side?' Mr Clarke's whole expression had changed. He had removed his spectacles and was staring at the bishop with undisguised hostility. From being a benign and placid ecclesiastic the stranger had become a forceful and energetic man of affairs. 'Did it seem possible to you that your interference might be of the greatest disservice to your own cause?'

'I have not interfered, sir. I have merely warned you of the suspicions you have aroused. It is my hope that you can explain your presence to Mr Galway.'

'And you do not perceive that a reproof is likely to reach you from Dublin Castle? These are troubled times, as you say, and there is sedition on every side. Is it likely that the government would neglect to send its agents to the threatened coast? Some—who knows?—might be disguised as catholic priests, men in whom the dissidents would confide. Others could be protestant clergy, attorneys on business, gentlemen intent on sea fishing. How can they succeed in their mission if arrested by every magistrate who suspects them?'

'Surely, sir,' said Mr Ludlow, 'their being arrested would

make them the more acceptable to the rebels?'

'A very intelligent comment, Mr Ludlow. I begin to wonder whether you are yourself exactly what you seem. May I ask, sir, how long you have been chaplain to the bishop?'

'He has been my chaplain,' said the bishop, 'for over a year and came to me with the strongest recommendation from a nobleman whose loyalty is beyond question.'

'No doubt, my lord. Mr Ludlow's reputation is well established. But what if this gentleman's real name were Smith or Jones?'

'Really, my lord!' exclaimed Ludlow. 'This is intolerable!'

'No more so than your suspicions about me!' This retort left Mr Clarke in possession of the field, his enemies in disarray. He went on to complete their discomfiture.

'I have not claimed, my lord, to be a secret agent from Dublin Castle. I merely point out that you have no proof that I am an enemy, nor proof indeed that Mr Ludlow is a friend. To that I add that you are in some danger of being made to look extremely foolish.'

'Foolish or not, I must ask you to remain here in Killala until noon tomorrow, at which hour you can explain yourself to Mr Galway. Do you agree to that?'

'Yes, my lord. I can stay so long without too much inconvenience. And now let me take my leave. Good evening to your lordship. Good evening, gentlemen.'

It was Mr Ludlow who saw him to the front door and came back with a look of bewilderment.

'He has gone, my lord. If he is still here at noon tomorrow we may conclude that he is indeed an agent on our side. If he vanishes or seeks to vanish before daybreak—as I think more likely—we shall know that he is an enemy agent. May I suggest, my lord, that it is our duty to watch the house where he is lodging and arrest him should he attempt to leave during the night?'

'I don't know,' replied the bishop hesitantly, 'I hardly

think—it is really very doubtful—and do we have men sufficiently trustworthy?'

'We have Tom, your coachman, my lord, and Larry of the post office.'

'One wants to do what is right . . . but are we justified in using force? We are men of peace, remember, and must be true to our cloth . . .'

By this time Delancey was eager to take his leave. He had not actually disobeyed orders in coming ashore but he had done so without Kerr's knowledge. He would look very foolish if Kerr changed his plans, deciding to sail that night, or else signalled for him to come aboard *Vulture*. There was nothing more he could do at Killala. His immediate duty was to return to his ship.

'Goodbye, my lord,' said Delancey. 'I am sorry to have been of so little use, and sorry to leave a problem unsolved. I hope to return here, however, and hear the end of the story.'

'Goodbye, Captain Delancey,' replied the bishop, 'I realise that you are not on your own. Thank you for acting your part so well. I look forward to your paying us another visit.'

It was dark by the time that Delancey reached the landing place but he knew that he had the perfect pilot in young David Stock. Launching his crazy boat again, the boy rowed off into the moonless night with complete confidence, chatting easily about the navigational hazards. Within the half hour they were alongside the *Spitfire*, Delancey having answered the lookout's challenge in such a way as to kill any ceremony on his coming aboard.

'Goodnight, David,' he called. 'Well done!'

It was a relief to hear after that from Partridge that there had been no signals from the *Vulture* and no sort of crisis on board his own ship. He turned in at once, knowing that Kerr would make sail as he had said, at daylight.

Delancey was called at four and so were all hands. The

anchor was hove short and all was ready for the gun and the signal, with men at the halliards and sheets and topmen already aloft. A faint light was appearing over the land and it would soon be daybreak.

Suddenly came the voice of the lookout on the forecastle, 'Boat ahoy! Keep clear. What do you want?'

Delancey could not hear the reply but went forward to see what was happening. There was just light enough for him to identify David Stock in his old fishing boat.

'All right, David,' he called. 'Bring your boat to the main entry and come aboard. Be quick, though. We shall be sailing in a few minutes.'

The boat bumped its way aft along the ship's side and some-one threw the boy a rope. An instant later David was on deck, just recognisable in the half-dark.

'Well, David?'

'Mr Ludlow was murdered last night, sir.'

'How—where?'

'He was stabbed, sir, with a knife, not far from where Mr Clarke was staying.'

'And Mr Clarke?'

'Gone, sir.'

'Did the bishop send you?'

'No, sir.'

'Why did you come?'

'To tell you, sir.'

'Thank you, David.' There was a pause and Delancey wondered what the boy was waiting for.

'Perhaps you had better go ashore again, David?'

'No, sir. I don't want to go back.'

'What, then?'

'I want to join your ship, sir.'

'Impossible, David, without your father's permission. If I accepted you, he would have no idea where you were. He and your mother would think you were drowned.'

'No, they wouldn't, sir. I left a note.' There was a touch of obstinacy in the boy's voice. He had made a decision and was not going back on it.

'Look, David, I can't accept you. But I shall be back here again in a few weeks' time and we can discuss the whole idea with your father. If he agrees, I shall take you on board as a volunteer. How will that satisfy you?'

'No, sir.'

'What do you mean 'no'? I am telling you what I have decided to do.'

'But it won't satisfy me. I want to join now.'

'Well, you can't. Be off with you!'

At that instant came the boom of a cannon on board the *Vulture*, followed by a chorus of protest from the seagulls and a booming echo from across the bay. Simultaneously came the signal to make sail.

'Acknowledge!' called Delancey. 'All hands, make sail!'

'Get the anchors up!' came the order and, 'Let fall the topsails!'

The *Spitfire* broke ground and was under way inside two minutes, fractionally ahead of the *Vulture* herself. Looking over in that direction, Delancey smiled for an instant and then gave an order to the helmsman, who repeated it. The ship began to gather way. Then Delancey realised that David was still on board.

'Quick, David,' he said. 'Into your boat!'

'I can't, sir.'

'And why not?'

'She sank, sir.'

Delancey strode to the ship's side and, looking aft, saw the last of that old craft in the *Spitfire*'s wake. David, he guessed, had himself knocked a hole in her and cut the painter, destroying what was almost his only possession in the world. Why had the boy done it? For the moment, however, David had won his point. He had wanted to stay on board and there was now no alternative. Delancey would not enter him as a member of the crew but would make him a guest and a temporary 'young gentleman'. He could be sent home from the next place at which the ship might call, perhaps Ballyshannon.

'Mr Heyworth!'

The more senior of the *Spitfire*'s two midshipmen came up to Delancey and touched his hat.

'This youngster is David Stock, who is to be with us for the next few days. Take him below and allot him a berth. See that he is issued with a hammock and bedding. He will mess with you and the others and join the starboard watch.'

'Aye, aye, sir.'

David disappeared in Heyworth's care and Delancey turned once more to handling the ship. He had now the new problem of informing Kerr what had happened. There was no combination of flags which would convey the message, 'Ludlow murdered—bishop's son on board.' He decided to wait his opportunity and was lucky to this extent that Kerr decided to drop anchor briefly in Sligo Bay, probably to call for the mail. Delancey lowered a boat and came aboard the *Vulture*, taking David with him. He made his report and Kerr questioned the boy for a few minutes, ascertaining that he was not a witness to the murder. He then talked with Delancey alone.

'It looks as if the bishop's theory about French spies disguised as clergy may be correct.'

'But do we know that, sir?' asked Delancey.

'Well, this fellow who calls himself Clarke is an impostor and Ludlow, who exposed him, is murdered. Killala may well be the place at which the French are to land.'

'With respect, sir, it is also possible that Ludlow was the French agent and that Clarke is on our side.'

'Dammit, I suppose that's true. . . .'

'In either event, sir, Killala may be the centre of the stage.'

'Yes, but not this early in the year. And there may be more than one landing, remember, or several feints and one in force.'

'Very true, sir.'

'So I shall continue to patrol northward as planned.'

'Aye, aye, sir. And the boy? Shall we send him home from here?'

'No. I shall write to the bishop as well as to Captain Ashley. But keep young David and see how he shapes as a seaman. He may become a useful midshipman. In the meanwhile—who knows?—we may be glad of a local pilot for Killala Bay.'

CHAPTER NINE

Revolt in Ireland

THE *Vulture* and *Spitfire* were once more at anchor in Sligo Bay but this time on their way south. It was the end of July and the two ships had been cruising for months on the west coast of Ireland, back and forth between Galway and Donegal. They had been into every inlet and visited every town from Westport to Buncrana. Delancey was entranced by the beauty of the coastline and the glimpses he had of the interior. As a Guernseyman, brought up in a small island, he had never seen in early life such an empty landscape, such great hillsides in the sunlight, silent save for the call of wildfowl. Here and there, widely scattered, were small groups of cottages. Still more scattered were the homes of the gentry, white-columned in wooded parks and approached by long avenues of trees. It was a country for hunting or fishing, for gardening or painting landscapes. Never would he forget, moreover, the hospitality he met with when ashore. He would find himself dining, from time to time, with a magistrate or clergyman and each host seemed more generous than the last. He was urged to make use of horses and sporting guns. He was asked to stay for the night—no, for the month—and told to look upon each mansion as his own. A number of dinner parties were spoilt for him by the fact that Captain Kerr was a fellow guest and regarded him with a malicious eye, hoping that he would in some way betray his humble origin. But Kerr did not accept every invitation and there were parties, luckily, from which he was therefore absent, and these could be very pleasant indeed.

Background to all this social life was a country in a state of civil war. There was relative peace in Sligo and Donegal, restless as the peasants may have been, but there was talk of actual fighting in Waterford and Kerry, with pitched battles at Enniscorthy and Wexford Bridge. Rumours were repeated about dark deeds perpetrated by the rebels on the one side, by Lord Lake's dragoons on the other; as also by the North Cork Militia. There were other tales again about French agents and invasion plans. How much should one believe? The one certain fact was that there was enough rebellion—and certainly enough talk about rebellion—to create an apparent opportunity for the French. Their spies would undoubtedly tell them of rebel forces needing only arms and ammunition. Even a small invading force could form the nucleus of a large native army. No one could doubt that this was the belief of the Irish leaders, men like Wolfe Tone or Napper Tandy, and none could question that this was the story the French would be told. They would hear less, perhaps, about the quarrels likely to occur among the Irish themselves and less still about the difficulties likely to arise between Irish catholics and French atheists. That French help was expected was certain. That the French would actually land was at least highly probable. It seemed, however, to Delancey that an invading force would land at Waterford or Kinsale, aiming to make contact with rebels who were actually in the field. That French agents had been active at Killala he knew for a fact but the knowledge they had gained there might well have led them to rule it out. It was, apart from that, rather remote. As a landing place Sligo seemed at least equally unsuitable if only for lack of population; and Mayo was, if anything, worse. There was no doubt in his mind that the regular appearance of British men-of-war had a calming, a steadying effect.

As Delancey paced his deck, admiring the bold outline of the

Dartry Mountains directly inland, the Ox Mountains further south, he knew that his crew could now be relied upon. He had worked them hard but they had also had the luxury of fresh meat and vegetables. The purser was ashore now and would return with sheep and chickens, with cheese and eggs. There was no sign of his longboat but he could see some sort of wherry approaching the *Vulture* under sail. Perhaps this would bring an invitation from the local magistrate, Mr Booth-Gore, or maybe new orders sent overland from Cork.

Ten minutes later *Vulture* made the signal for *Spitfire's* captain to come on board. The gig was already in the water and Delancey lost no time in obeying the order. Kerr received him as usual, looking him up and down without enthusiasm.

'Good morning, captain. I have just received an urgent letter from Captain Ashley. I learn from this that the French have two expeditions fitting out; both, it is thought, for Ireland. One is collected at Brest under Commodore Bompart, with 3000 troops embarked; the other is collected at Rochefort under Commodore Savary, with something over 1000 soldiers. This, anyway, is what we are told. Our agents failed to discover, however, the point or points at which these forces are to disembark. We are merely told to expect them on the Irish coast.'

'And what part, sir, are we to play in thwarting the French plan?'

'We are to remain on the coast, reporting back to Cork should the enemy appear. In the event of rebels assembling at any particular point, as if expecting a French landing, we are to inform Captain Ashley at once.'

'Aye, aye, sir.'

'Interpreting these orders, I propose to quit this bay. I do not want to be trapped here by superior forces. I shall patrol, therefore, between Broad Haven and Malinbeg. If and when the French are seen, I shall send you to Cork and will myself keep the enemy in sight.'

'Aye, aye, sir.'

'You look doubtful, captain.'

'Well, sir, I wonder how the next message sent overland will reach you.'

'The harbour master here will be told to forward all letters to Broad Haven.'

'Very good, sir.'

'You still look doubtful.'

'I am wondering how news will reach you if the French should land in Lough Swilly.'

'The harbour-master at Buncrana will send a message to Donegal. I think, however, that Lough Swilly is in little danger, being too far from Dublin. We sail with this evening's tide and I'll hope to see *Spitfire* smartly under way. Your crew is better than it was but there is still room for improvement.'

No further despatches came from Cork but there were rumours everywhere about French landings to be expected. Nothing happened, however, until the last week in August. It was the season arranged for the Bishop of Killala's diocesan synod; the annual meeting of his parish clergy, numbering about a dozen. They came together on August 21st, some arriving late that evening, and held their first conclave on the morning of the next day.

Handicapped somewhat for lack of a chaplain—for there had been insufficient time to replace Mr Ludlow—the Bishop had himself to write out copies of the agenda, which began with the vexed topic of church schools. All was ready at the appointed hour when a note reached his lordship from the collector of customs. It said briefly that several unidentified men-of-war had been sighted. Concluding that these would be some British cruisers and hoping that the *Spitfire* was one of them, he entered his dining room, where the meeting was to be held, and called the synod to order. After an opening prayer, he announced the first subject for discussion and invited Mr Carpenter to enlarge on the views he had already outlined a year before.

'My lord,' Mr Carpenter began, 'we all feel . . .'

Mr Carpenter's voice died away at the sound of gunfire. Before he could resume there was a further concussion, enough to break one of the windows. The bishop rang a bell near the fireplace, meaning to ask his servant what was happening. Before he could do so, however, the door burst open and a terrified parlourmaid appeared.

'It's the French here, m'lord, with killings and murder!'

From the village came the sound of musketry and of orders being shouted, of horses cantering and women screaming. When the manservant appeared, the bishop told him to bar the outer doors.

'We'll hold the castle,' he announced bravely, 'until the yeomanry arrive!'

'The yeomanry fired a few shots, m'lord, but galloped off before the French could fire back. There are French soldiers in the castle already!'

Shrieks of alarm could be heard from the hall. Within seconds a tall French officer strode into the room and announced that all present were prisoners and must leave at once. Sword in hand and speaking tolerable English, he directed them down the stairs and shut them, for the time being, in the scullery. Mrs Stock, her children and servants, were driven in afterward and they were told that General Humbert, commander of the invading army, would use the castle as his headquarters.

The scullery had one small window overlooking the harbour and by climbing up on the sink they could just look out of it. Towards evening the bishop saw to his surprise that the French men-of-war were leaving the harbour under sail. Later he was called to the same window by someone tapping it with a stick. It turned out to be the coachman, Tom, who had been in the village when the French arrived.

'Could you get through the window, my lord?' he called up.

'No,' said the bishop, 'but my boys could. Is there no one on watch?'

'Not this side there isn't.'

'What's happening?'

'Well, my lord, there are French soldiers here under General Humbert. They are not behaving too badly for they have been told not to plunder.'

'I must send warning, Tom. Could you bring me paper, pen and ink?'

'I'll try, my lord.'

'Do that, then, Tom!'

It took the coachman some time to find writing materials in the village. He ended by robbing the school after dark, but when he got back it was found he had brought no means of making a light. It was an anxious wait till daylight, when the bishop could start to write his letters. Quickly he wrote three, one for Broad Haven, one for Sligo and a third for Newport. Two of his sons were small enough to be passed up and squeezed through the scullery window. In the cold light of dawn they made off with Tom by a covered lane. All three letters were on their way before General Humbert found better and more secure accommodation for his prisoners.

No further messages left the castle and two of the letters actually sent seem to have miscarried. The only letter to be delivered was that taken by Tom, who managed to reach Broad Haven on a borrowed horse. Three hours later Captain Kerr received this letter on board the *Vulture*, thirty miles away to the westward.

It was dated from Killala on 23rd August and read as follows:

Sir,

It is with regret that I write to inform you of a French landing at this place. Four frigates yesterday dropped anchor off

Kilcummin Head and landed over 1000 soldiers under General Humbert together with four cannon and spare weapons for such of the deluded Irish rebels as may rally to the green flag he has hoisted above his headquarters established in my house. I presume that his next object will be the capture of Ballina. The frigates sailed again yesterday on their return voyage, it is said, to France. According to their Commodore, Savary, there are other ships to be expected with a larger body of troops. Being virtually a prisoner I have had great difficulty in finding means to deliver this letter but have at length entrusted this to a reliable servant who hopes to find a horse at Ballycastle, all mine being taken by the French.

I have the honour to be, sir,
Your obedient servant,
Killala ✠

The Senior Officer,
H. M. Ships,
Broad Haven.

The Bishop was quite correct in stating that other troops were on their way, for Admiral Bompart's expedition was indeed assembling at Brest and Savary was going to Rochefort to embark a second detachment. What he did not report and could not know was that Savary had sailed with one other ship, the *Hercule* of 74 guns, commanded by Captain L'Héritier. Her voyage had been delayed by the loss of her foretopmast and she was approaching Killala Bay during the night of the 23rd, missing Savary in the darkness and making the coast of Mayo at daybreak.

Warned by Dr Stock's letter Captain Kerr sailed at once from Broad Haven, bound for Killala Bay. The result was that the *Vulture* and *Spitfire* were on the same course as the *Hercule* but about twelve miles astern. When Kerr first sighted the

Hercule she was entering Killala Bay with the expectation, no doubt, of joining Savary's squadron. The bay was empty, however, and the green flag over the castle was the only clue to what had happened. Savary had landed his troops on the west side of the bay but L'Héritier dropped anchor off Inishcrone, intending to land his troops (300 of them) at that point. As he prepared to do so he received a message from Colonel Charost, telling him that Humbert was marching on Ballina.

The detachment of troops on board the *Hercule* was commanded by Colonel Michaud, who realised that he could as easily reach Ballina from Inishcrone. His men were landed before midday but the additional arms and accoutrements for the Irish rebels took some hours to put ashore. More time was spent in remounting the *Hercule's* lower deck guns, some of them having been struck in the hold to make room for the soldiers.

By the early evening the *Hercule* was ready to sail again, her boats hoisted inboard and her mission performed. It was only then that Captain L'Héritier made an important discovery.

Off Kilcummin Head, about eight miles away, Captain Kerr was watching the French ship of the line through his telescope. Knowing that the other French ships had sailed again after landing their troops, he could fairly assume that this latecomer would follow suit. There was nothing he could do to interfere but he would be wrong to leave the scene until he could complete his report, stating the direction in which the French 74 had gone. He would then send *Spitfire* to Cork with that information, while he himself followed the enemy in *Vulture*. He once more made the signal for the captain of *Spitfire* to come aboard.

It was a fine summer evening, the sea a sparkling blue, the nor' westerly breeze was tending to die away and all was quiet ashore. There was fighting, most probably, round Ballina but Killala was silent under its green flag. Ireland might be in a state of rebellion, with the catholic peasantry joining General Humbert in their thousands, but nothing of this could be seen or heard at Killala. There was some boat activity around the French man-of-war and Kerr guessed that water was being brought from the shore. With troops on board she might well have used up much of her water on the voyage from France. From any other point of view, said Kerr to himself, she would have done better to sail before now, using the last of the ebb and maybe the last of the breeze. She was in no danger, however, and probably had an Irish pilot on board. The two distant sloops her captain could afford to ignore. They would be no match for even a frigate.

Captain Kerr welcomed Delancey with his usual air of patronage:

'You will realise, captain, that the French have landed in Ireland and are probably advancing towards Castlebar. That is Lord Lake's concern. The frigates from which the first troops landed are on their way back to France—or so I should suppose—but this one late arrival is still at anchor and will no doubt follow within the next few hours, assisted by moonlight and the advice, very likely, of some local Irishman. I shall follow in the hope of contacting our cruisers and you will sail for Cork with my report of what has taken place. I think proper to delay your sailing until this last French ship has actually left the bay.'

'Your report would read better, sir, if it ended with an account of how this last ship came to be destroyed while at anchor.'

'Are you out of your mind, sir? Do you think that I have failed to consider every possible plan of attack? Have you ever heard of two sloops attacking a ship of the line? I confess that it is vexing to see an enemy ship at anchor in a British harbour. But there is nothing we can do. We can inform our senior officers, to be sure. We can try to keep her in sight. But to close with that ship would be virtual suicide. Come, Mr Delancey, you can see that for yourself.'

'I see that, sir, but I can also see something else. That French ship is not merely at anchor. She is aground.'

'How do you know, sir?'

'You may remember, sir, that I have a pilot on board. Young David Stock knows every inch of this coast. He tells me that she'll be aground for the next four hours but will have taken no harm on that part of the shore. There are no rocks there and the sea is calm. But she won't make sail until after nine. I submit, sir, that she is a sitting target.'

'Do you mean—seriously—?'

'Yes, sir, for a fireship attack.'

'But no fireship has been used in living memory!'

'I know that, sir. But the *Spitfire* has been designed for this special service. Such an occasion may come only once in a lifetime.'

'But what if you miss? I shall have sacrificed the *Spitfire* and with nothing to show for it.'

'And what if you let the Frenchman escape? You will be told that you had the chance to destroy her and preferred to do nothing.'

'Exactly. It's damned awkward, whatever I do. It's easy for you—no, I don't mean that, it will be a hellish task—but *I* have to take the responsibility. Make a mistake and they hold it against you for years. What the devil should I decide?'

Delancey looked at Kerr with interest. The aristocratic poise had gone. He was pacing the cabin and biting his nails. Suddenly he paused as if struck by a new idea:

'But nobody need know that this damned ship *is* aground— not unless I report it!'

'The fact, sir, will be known to everybody in Inishcrone and Killala'.

'That's true, by God!'

'Look, sir, time is passing. If I'm to destroy that ship before she is afloat, I shall have to begin now. If it helps you to decide, let me say this: when in doubt, it's better to do something than nothing.'

'I suppose that is right. Very well, then. We attack. But what is the *Vulture* to do?'

'Follow in, sir, and finish off the enemy by gunfire.'

'Shall I pick up your boats after the attack has been made?'

'Thank you, sir. I think, however, that we shall go straight on and make for the beach. Perhaps you will be good enough to fetch us afterwards? I could also make good use of an extra boat.'

'Very well. Now you will want to decide on the exact hour.'

'Yes, sir. I shall aim to hit the target at nine, hoping it will be dark enough by then. It can't be earlier or I shall be seen and it can't be later or she'll be afloat. With your concurrence I propose to sail past Lenadoon Point, as if returning to Sligo. Then I shall go about and round the Point again at 7.30. That will leave me with six miles to go under easy sail and with the flood tide. I shall keep in close to the land, merge with the background and hope not to be noticed.

'And the *Vulture*?'

'Might I suggest that you appear off Ross Point and distract the enemy with rockets and gunfire? If his lookout men are watching you they are less likely to notice us'

'Very well. I shall make a dummy attack on Killala and hope to draw the fire of the enemy. It looks to me as if they have mounted some guns ashore.'

'Thank you, sir. At 8 o'clock if you please, and with still more noise at 8.45. The more noise the better! Shall we compare our watches?'

'Yes. It lacks ten minutes to six.'

'Thank you, sir. And may I leave David Stock with you?'

'I don't think I need him.'

'He is merely a passenger, sir, embarked without his father's consent. I don't feel justified in risking his life.'

'Oh, I see what you mean. Yes, he had best stay with me, in

safety. I wish you the very best of good fortune!'

They shook hands at parting and Delancey felt more friendly towards Kerr, knowing that the young man was more at fault in manner than in his actual behaviour. He told his boat's crew to row him back to the *Spitfire*. There was a great deal to do and all too little time in which to do it.

As soon as he had been piped aboard, Delancey told Partridge to muster all hands. Within a few minutes the boatswain reported all present to Partridge, who reported in turn to the captain. Standing at the break of the quarterdeck, Delancey looked over his men with a critical eye. They looked better than they had looked at first. These were the men he had to lead into danger. Here were the men whose lives he might have to sacrifice. . . .The least he could do was to explain why their sacrifice—and that of the ship herself—was justified.

'You all know by now that the French have landed troops here at Killala. Their frigates have gone back to France for more. But one ship, a 74, put in here after the others had gone and landed the troops she had on board. She is aground, however, and will not float again, her captain realises, until nine this evening. What her captain does not know, but what we know, is that she will never float again at all. We who serve the King do not like to see an enemy ship in a British port save as a prize. Still less do we like to see an enemy ship leave a British port undamaged. My intention is to destroy that French ship. You will all know that the *Vulture* and *Spitfire* are no match for a 74. But this is a fireship and ours is that very rare situation in which a fireship can be used. We are faced by a sitting target of sufficient importance.

'I want you all to take a good look at her. You will see that she is aground on the east side of Killala Bay, her bows pointing nearly due south, her starboard broadside bearing on Ross Point, her port broadside bearing on the shore at close range. From our point of view this position has one advantage and one drawback. Our advantage is that we can make our attack from the north without coming under fire from her main armament. The drawback is that her stern presents only a small target, compelling us to steer this ship up to the last moment. The weather conditions are suitable but with rather less wind than I should like. With the shore so close I do not expect heavy losses. We shall hope, moreover, to end on the beach with our personal possessions, with the knowledge that we have done our duty and with the prospect of receiving head-money for an enemy 74 destroyed. The sum to be divided will not be as great as we should gain from her capture. As against that, there are only about 50 of us to share what there is. I plan first of all to sail out of sight past Lenadoon Point—that headland over there—so that the enemy will think we have been sent off with a message. The *Vulture* will remain in sight and is to make a dummy attack on Killala, enough to attract attention and give the French something else to look at. Then we shall go about, return in the failing light and make our attack after dark. Good luck to you all, and now—all hands make sail!'

While passing out of sight, from the enemy's point of view, the final arrangements were made. Sending for the carpenter, boatswain, gunner, sailmaker and purser, Delancey ordered the construction of a breastwork forward of the wheel. The framework would consist of gratings and spars but it had to be packed with something more solid.

'Use casks of meat and bread from the hold,' he added, 'and finish it off with spare canvas and hammocks.' The purser was shocked.

'We can't waste provisions, sir! Surely, water casks will serve your purpose?'

'Look, Mr Holt, I'm going to destroy the entire ship, provisions and all, so don't worry about your accounts. Water casks are just what I don't want on deck. They would tend to put the fire out.'

'Well, sir, I suppose you know best. After a lifetime, however, of economising stores and accounting for expenditure this idea of destruction is hard to take—very hard indeed—but I'll have the casks swayed up.'

'Now, Mr Shepherd,' said Delancey to the gunner, 'I want two carronades mounted in the bows, to fire through another breastwork, with plenty of ready-to-use ammunition. Mr Gillingham, examine and check all the boats and have them ready to lower. All will be towed astern when we go into action.'

There was frantic activity for the next hour or two. By that time the *Spitfire* was round the point and unseen by the enemy. Delancey presently gave the order to go about. Light was failing and the breeze from the northwest was freshening slightly. He found himself wondering whether he would ever see daylight again. After watching what might well be his last sunset, a pale yellow fading slowly to grey, Delancey called his officers into the cabin for a final conference, leaving the purser in momentary charge of the deck. Besides Partridge and the two master's mates—Ewins and Fairbrother—there was Shepherd, the gunner, Gillingham the boatswain, Browning the carpenter and, finally, the two midshipmen, Heyworth and Travers.

'Well, gentlemen, you all heard what I said to the ship's company and you all saw that French 74 on its sandbank. You all know what we have to do and by what hour it has to be done. We are to destroy that ship before she floats again at about nine tonight. We can rely on the *Vulture* for active co-operation in distracting the enemy. We cannot rely on the local inhabitants for help when our task is done and we reach the shore. Remember that Killala is in French hands and that many of the inhabitants will side with the enemy—at least for the time being. We must land ready to fight.

'Our ship, remember, was designed and is equipped for our present purpose. I shall put *Spitfire* alongside the enemy and blow her up at the proper time. Our approach must be in complete silence, the object being to close the enemy before we are seen. When we are discovered the French will open fire with their stern chasers and we shall return the fire. I shall cease fire, however, at a quarter to nine. For the purpose of this attack the ship's company will be divided between five boats, to leave the ship successively on my orders.

'The first boat to go will be the one we have borrowed from the *Vulture*. Mr Ewins and Mr Browning will take six armed men in this boat and load spare arms, ammunition, gunpowder, blankets and personal possessions. Beach the boat at the nearest point and stand guard over her. The second boat will be commanded by Mr Partridge with Mr Travers and will carry 16 men, fully armed. Your task, Mr Partridge, will be to take up position on the south side of Inishcrone, preventing any French or Irish interference from that direction. The third boat will be the launch with Mr Fairbrother and Mr Gillingham, manned by 12 men, fully armed, whose task will be to take the French survivors prisoner as they come ashore. The fourth boat will be the five-oared cutter with 10 men, fully armed, under Mr Shepherd and Mr Heyworth, who will take up position on the north side of the village. I shall myself take the gig. Mr Partridge, please detail the men to their several boats. Mr Ewins, please check the boat stores. Mr Fairbrother, have the bow chasers manned and ready for action. Mr Shepherd, distribute the arms. Mr Gillingham, Mr Browning, come with me.'

As the *Spitfire* approached Lenadoon Point Delancey told the boatswain and carpenter about rigging the grapnels, weakening the masts and preparing to cut the weather shrouds. Preparations were mostly complete when the *Spitfire* rounded the point and began her run down the east side of the bay.

It was growing dark and the following wind was ideal for the attack as planned. It was a little before 7.30 and Delancey shortened sail, taking in the topsails (as more visible) and coming in under the forecourse and spanker with a leadsman in the chains under orders not to sing out unless the water shoaled to five fathoms. It was essential to hug the shore so as to merge the ship's outline with the headland but it would be fatal to touch bottom and lose time. There was just light enough to see the *Vulture* as she approached Ross Point. Delancey, standing beside the wheel, felt in his pocket to make sure that he had flint and steel, tinder and fuse. There was a loaded musket in the gig and two pistols in his belt. He racked his brain to think what he might have forgotten, then turned sharply to find that Partridge was beside him.

'All well, sir. We have as good a chance as we could hope for. But that ship's stern is a small target, sir. The odds must be against us.'

'Not with me at the wheel, Mr Partridge. I shall be here until the two ships touch.'

'But that is to kill yourself, sir!'

'No, I shall escape in the gig.'

'Which by then will be sunk. You mustn't do this, sir. Leave it to me—or let me stay with you.'

'I have issued my orders, Mr Partridge, and I expect them to be obeyed. I don't want the survivors from this French ship to join up with the French troops at Killala. It is your task to prevent that. Should I fall, moreover, it will still be your task to act against the enemy. I have no other commissioned officer and we must not be so placed that the same shot could kill us both. So you will take the second boat. I have just remembered something, however. I want a barrel of gunpowder in the gig. Instruct Mr Shepherd to see to it.' It was only an excuse to get rid of old Partridge, but it worked.

Delancey looked at his watch. It was nearly a quarter past seven. The *Spitfire* was approaching Lenadoon Point, just visible to leeward. At that moment came a muffled shout from the forecastle, an exclamation from the leadsman and a sickening jar through the ship's fabric. The swaying motion of the deck had stopped. The noise of the water along the ship's side died away. Such was the shock that Delancey felt as if his heart had stopped beating. With an awful feeling of disaster and finality he knew that the worst had happened. There was no room for doubt or hope. The *Spitfire* had run aground.

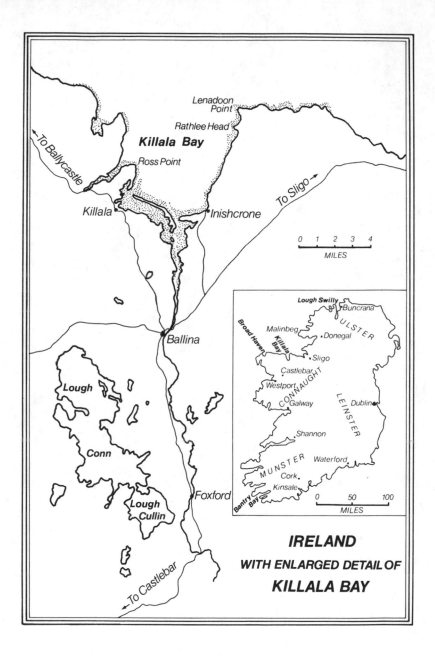

Killala Bay

To Ballycastle

Lenadoon Point

Rathlee Head

Ross Point

Killala Inishcrone

To Sligo

0 1 2 3 4
MILES

Ballina

Lough

Conn

Lough Cullin

Foxford

To Castlebar

Lough Swilly Buncrana

Malinbeg Donegal ULSTER

Broad Haven Killala Bay

Sligo

Castlebar

Westport CONNAUGHT

Galway LEINSTER Dublin

Shannon

MUNSTER Waterford

Cork

Kinsale

Bantry Bay

0 50 100
MILES

IRELAND

WITH ENLARGED DETAIL OF

KILLALA BAY

☆ ☆

CHAPTER TEN

The End of the Spitfire

THE SUCCESS of the attack, as planned, was to be a matter of timing. A delay of 15 minutes would be enough to wreck the whole attempt. Once the French 74 were afloat she could swing round and bring her whole battery to bear on the *Spitfire*, blowing her to pieces as she approached. A further effect of any delay would be to waste the effect of *Vulture*'s dummy attack. *Spitfire* was on a sandbank and would probably float off it as the tide rose. There was no danger of her being stranded, only the danger of her being late.

Thinking quickly, Delancey knew that he had two advantages. First of all, he had allowed ten minutes extra in case of accidents. In the second place, his ship was expendable and was not on her way to fight an ordinary action. The first thing was to take sail off her before a topmast went over the side. He gave orders to that effect and then shouted, 'All broadside guns over the side! Quickly! Jump to it! Move as you never moved before!'

He himself led a group which tore at the aftermast carronades, hacked away their breach ropes, heaved the guns off their slides and tumbled them through the ports.

'Carriages as well,' he gasped. 'Ammunition, too.'

He could hear splashes as the guns went overboard, all except the bow guns and the two guns on the forecastle, four in all.

'Lower all boats!' he called out—they were ready to lower and would in any case have been lowered very shortly.

What else could go? He thought of the stores but realised that there was no time for that. Easiest weight to remove was that of the crew.

'Man all boats but Number Two,' he ordered, and then had another inspiration. 'Mr Partridge, jettison all anchors and cables.'

In other circumstances he would have taken a boat to discover what depth of water there was ahead, but there was no time for that. If the sandbank they had struck was more than an isolated spit, the battle was lost.

It was the anchors going which turned the scales. Delancey felt the deck alive beneath his feet. There was a quivering and a shudder and the *Spitfire* slid gently forward into deeper water. Some nightmare minutes passed as the crew scrambled on board again, leaving the boats in the water, and further time was lost in making sail. When the ship began to make headway at last Delancey looked at his watch, fearing the worst. They had lost twenty minutes, ten of which he had allowed for. Could he make up for lost time? The one thing he dared not do was to come any closer to Lenadoon Point. As against that the ship was lighter now and perhaps a little faster.

From the moment of striking the sandbank, Delancey was haunted by the knowledge that the fault had been his. There had been no error of navigation, the sands having shifted since the chart was made. He had not been mistaken in that way. His error had been to discard his pilot. David Stock could have warned him about that confounded sandbank. David could equally have told him how near he could go to Lenadoon Point and how close again to Rathlee Head. Now David was on board the wrong ship, the *Vulture*, the sloop with the easy task of distracting attention. And why? Because he, Delancey, had wanted to keep the boy out of danger. Oh, there were excuses enough—the youngster's age and civilian status, the anxiety of the bishop (with troubles enough of his own), the boy's possible future—but the mistake had still been made and might well prove to have been fatal.

The time had come to turn southwards into the bay and he gave the necessary orders. As the ship steadied on her new course the wind was freshening, perhaps enough to clip five minutes off the time he had allowed for his approach to the target. He might be only a few minutes late after all. Despite the turmoil caused by the grounding, the ship was now in pretty good order with boats towed astern in their right order. There was a steady quartermaster at the wheel, Jim Malling, and there was a boy at his side to take messages, a rather bright fifteen-year-old called Ned Walker. Slowly the *Spitfire* was coming abreast of Rathlee Head. Delancey now looked at his watch and saw that it was 7.45. There was some fading light to the westward but no trace of moon. He could as yet see nothing of the target ship, hidden against the land, and nothing of the *Vulture*. He was in position, however, and only a few minutes behind time. If the wind held, he might still hope to hit the target as planned.

'First boat away!' was Delancey's first order and Ned dashed off to convey the order to Mr Ewins.

The borrowed boat from the *Vulture* was hauled alongside, manned and pushed off in a matter of three minutes. There went his own belongings and instruments together with the ship's papers and log.

Something about this discarding process made him suddenly feel afraid. He had never regarded himself as a hero. He had never before volunteered for any specially dangerous mission. What on earth had possessed him to do so now? Why had he planned the operation? Why had he left himself with the suicidal role? The trouble was that he had considered the problem in the abstract. He had known what the right move was, as in chess. He knew what further moves should follow, one after another. He knew that someone had to remain at the wheel. He also knew that the captain should be the last man to leave a doomed ship. It was only now, alone in the darkness, that he had come to realise all the implications. The captain should stay to the last—but *he* was the captain! It had been easy to decide upon a plan. Now he was coming to grasp the fact that he had sacrificed himself as part of the plan, just as a chess player will sacrifice a pawn. He shivered, wondering whether he had the courage to go through with it. Why didn't he take Partridge's advice? There was no turning back—the Frenchman's masts were just coming in sight with cobweb rigging against the darkening sky.

'Keep on target,' he said to the helmsman.

The silence of the night was suddenly broken by the jarring sound of a gun. Delancey feared for a moment that the *Spitfire* had been seen but realised almost at once that it was the *Vulture* that had fired. It must be 8 o'clock.

'Second boat away!' he called and the boy ran off to tell Mr Partridge.

There was a further burst of activity ending with the words, just audible, 'Shove off!'

Odd to think that he might never see Partridge again and that they had never even said goodbye. Discarding the boats was rather like preparation for death; making a last will and testament, giving away possessions, expressing one's last wishes. Could he change his plan even now?

Vulture fired a rocket at this point. It seemed to rise quite slowly and then burst, lighting Killala village for a moment. The rumble of the sloop's broadside followed, echoing across the bay. Having seen their point of aim, the gun captains had let fly. But what would they be firing àt? At rocks along the shore? But the French had mounted some guns there, he had been told. They could be, and probably were, the targets being engaged. He hoped that the cottages would be spared.

Shortly afterwards he again saw the *Vulture*'s gun flashes and heard the rumble a few seconds later. She must be five miles away, clean out of the French ship's range but plainly visible and doing everything possible to attract attention. Would the French captain be clever enough to conclude that this was a dummy operation and that he ought to look in another direction?

Another rocket lit the landscape round Ross Point and Delancey, seeing his watch face by its light, called out, 'Third boat away!'

Young Ned scurried off once more. There was a minute or two of hurried effort and then Delancey knew that Fairbrother had gone. There should be ten men left with Shepherd and Heyworth, mostly manning the bow chasers. The French ship was clearly visible now, perhaps a mile away, and it seemed impossible that *Spitfire* could still be unseen. The moon should have risen by now but it was hidden by clouds. The conditions for a fireship attack were perfect.

The situation changed abruptly with the firing of a rocket from the French ship of the line. It flew just east of north and burst nearly overhead, revealing the *Spitfire* in pitiless detail. The French may not have recognised her as a fireship, but they had seen enough. They engaged their assailant with two stern-chasers.

'Open fire!' Delancey shouted to Mr Shepherd.

The first French rounds were wide and high but their aim improved as the range lessened. Delancey heard a crash forward and knew that the forecastle was hit and the bowsprit probably damaged. Another shot fell amidships and bounced into the breastwork which covered *Spitfire*'s wheel.

The *Spitfire*'s bow-chasers replied, hitting the Frenchman's stern, but one of them was silenced at that point. Delancey could hear the crash as the gun overturned, the scream of a man wounded and the groaning of another man, possibly trapped under the gun itself.

He realised, with a shock of horror, that he might have to set light to the ship with wounded men still on board. He had not thought of that possibility, the idea of which made him choke. And yet he must continue firing until the last possible moment.

The French fire was heavier now—some more guns must have been shifted aft, perhaps firing through the cabin windows. Another round crashed into the barricade, demolishing half of it.

With ten minutes still to go—the longest ten minutes of his life—Delancey held grimly on course while French cannon balls raked his ship. His solitary gun replied but he could not see with what effect. Any moment a shot could hit the wheel. . . .

A series of hammer blows hit what was left of the barricade and Delancey realised that he was under musketry fire. There was now only five minutes to go. Taking the wheel from the helmsman, he sent the man forward with orders for the remaining gun to cease fire and for the men to run aft. The boy who had been his messenger then doubled forward as previously instructed, pouring oil along the deck to leeward and a train of gunpowder amidships leading to the bags of powder attached to the masts.

The deck was now under heavier small arms fire and Heyworth was killed on his way aft. Shepherd had been wounded but reached the wheel with three of his men. The former helmsman was so far unhurt and Delancey told him to cut the last of the windward shrouds. He had only dealt with the mainmast when he too fell, his axe sliding across the deck and ending with a thud on the lee scuppers.

'Fourth boat away!' yelled Delancey and saw Shepherd, two men and the boy go over the ship's side. Except for the wounded (heaven help them) Delancey knew that he was on his own.

The *Spitfire* was coming up on the seaward side of the French ship, raked by her stern chasers and swept by musket shot. Any moment the fireship might receive a shot which would explode her magazine and blow both ships to smithereens. Luckily, however, the French ship's stern chasers had been firing high, aiming to cripple her opponent. Both foresail and spanker had been shot to ribbons but enough canvas remained to keep the ship under way. Just as the *Spitfire*'s flying jib-boom overlapped the Frenchman's stern Delancey spun the wheel so as to swing his bow to port. There was a grinding crash as the *Spitfire*'s bow hit the Frenchman round about the mizzen chains.

The shock knocked Delancey off his feet leaving him bruised and winded. Recovering, he snatched the slow match which he had had placed near the wheel over a tub of water, blew on it and touched off the powder train. The flame raced forward over the deck and there was an explosion at the foot of each mast. For an awful moment it looked as if all three would survive but then, quite slowly, the mainmast went over the side, entangling itself with the French ship's spanker boom. As slowly again the foremast followed suit, crashing fairly across the Frenchman's quarterdeck. Staggering and dizzy, choked with smoke and coughing in the fumes, Delancey realised dimly that he had hit the target. The two ships were locked together and one of them was ablaze. The small arms fire had ceased, its place being taken by the crackle of the flames. The time had come when he could properly abandon ship.

At that instant a figure appeared from nowhere and took him by the arm.

'This way, sir!' a voice shouted and he found himself being steered towards the main entry port on the windward side.

A strong arm helped him down the ladder and another received him in the gig. He tumbled into the boat and heard the oars grind desperately in the rowlocks as the *Spitfire* was swiftly left astern. As he recovered, rubbing the smoke out of his eyes,

he recognised the men who had brought him away—young
Teesdale and Tanner, the gunner's mate. He was too ex-
hausted at the moment to wonder how they came to be there.
He merely felt with relief that the gig was pulling away from the
scene of the action.

Mingled with his relief, however, was a feeling that something was wrong. How long had passed since he quitted the
ship? Over five minutes, perhaps nearly ten. If all had gone according to plan there should have been a terrific explosion by
now. The firing had died away and there was little to be heard
but the splash of the oars. Raising himself with a muttered
oath, he looked back at the ships astern. The light of the flames
had died away but there was a plume of vapour over the
Spitfire's deck. He could just distinguish the distant shouting of
orders, suggesting that the situation was under control. There
could be no doubt about it. The fire had been extinguished.

'Vast pulling,' he said, surprised to find his voice as hoarse
and feeble as it turned out to be. The oars lay still and he sat for
a moment with his head in his hands.

'We shall have to go back,' he said finally. 'Pull, stroke. Back
water, bow.'

The men obeyed but Tanner asked why.

'They put the fire out,' Delancey explained wearily. 'That
damned Frenchman is afloat by now, free to escape as soon as
they have cut away the tangle. Give way, both.'

They were making too much noise and Delancey, tearing off
his shirt, made the two seamen muffle their oars. The worst
part of the situation was that the French captain would now
claim that he had captured the *Spitfire*. She might be brought
into a French port with the British ensign under the tricolour.
This could be the fate of the first King's ship of which he had
been given the command. . . . Tired as he was, he had to think
clearly and act quickly.

'Listen. We have a barrel of gunpowder in the bows and I

have slow match, tinder, flint and steel. I mean to tie this barrel, fuse lit, to that French ship's rudder. The French will be too busy with the wreckage to see us coming. Then we'll row round her bows, putting the ship between us and the explosion.'

'Beg pardon, sir,' said Tanner, 'Won't this one barrel touch off the rest in both ships?'

'No. It won't do much more than blow her rudder off and maybe start a leak.'

He could not explain then that a confined space is essential to a really destructive explosion. The effect of his one barrel would be mostly wasted in the air. It would do more good between the two ships but that was too risky. Too risky! As if his preferred plan could be thought safe. . . . Still, he could picture the scene on that French ship's deck. The captain's first thought would have been to extinguish the blaze in the *Spitfire*. His men would have used her foremast as a bridge but it would not have been easy and some of his boarders might have hung back. He would have had lines of men passing buckets and others trying to smother the blaze with wet sailcloth. Then there would be all the wreckage to clear and the mast to shift. There would also be the mizzen to re-rig and the spanker boom to replace. There would be work for another half-hour at least. The chance he had to take was that of someone looking over the stern while, say, replacing the ensign staff. By a lucky chance, however, the moon was still hidden. The gig would not be visible beyond a cable's distance. Any sound made, moreover, would probably be drowned by the noise being made on board the ship herself.

'Ship oars,' said Delancey, 'and hand that barrel aft.'

For the next twenty minutes, as the gig neared the French 74, Delancey was busy with slow match and bung hole, setting the fuse for ten minutes. Then he lit another length of match and cocked his musket, checked his pistols and loosened his sword in its sheath. Even if they were seen, he had an idea of what to do in the last resort.

As they neared the enemy ship the noise steadily increased. There came the sound of sawing and hammering, shouting and running. One voice came over more loudly than the rest and Delancey pictured the French captain driving his men with relentless determination. Feeling like a rat in a trap, sweating and swearing, he would want to be out of that cursed bay before daylight. All the other Frenchmen were jabbering too—they had no sense of discipline, these revolutionaries—and there seemed little chance of Delancey's gig being either seen or heard.

There was still a hundred yards to go and Delancey suddenly saw where his present plan was going to fail. There was a rough platform slung over the French ship's stern and a man was plugging a shot hole—one made by a cannon ball from the *Spitfire*. It was just above the rudder casing and Delancey knew exactly what the carpenter's mate would be doing. He would be hammering in a wooden plug, the size of the shot (carpenters had a selection of these ready for use) and then nailing over it a square patch of lead. It was not a difficult task in the ordinary way and would take about ten minutes.

Delancey had to think quickly again. He could shoot the man at short range but not without giving the alarm. He could wait for the man to finish and go. He could try to kill the fellow quietly with his sword. . . . Looking at the sky, Delancey decided against waiting. There was a break in the clouds and there would be moonlight quite soon. The sword thrust would not do—the man seemed to be out of reach. Then he had a better idea. The carpenter's mate, he could see, was busy with the sheet lead. He steered the boat alongside the rudder and came into position below the platform.

'Fini?' he called, 'Descendez en bateau!'

What more natural than to send a boat round to inspect the damage? Delancey thanked heaven for his Guernsey French. The young carpenter showed no surprise, for one. Pocketing his nails and pushing the hammer into the waistband of his trousers, he slid down a rope and into the bows of the boat, all without saying a word. He then found himself looking into the muzzle of Delancey's pistol.

'Silence!' was the only order that followed.

At a gesture from Delancey young Teesdale tied the Frenchman's wrists and ankles and gagged him with a kerchief. Then the gig was turned round with her stern against the ship's rudder and Delancey lashed his barrel to the upper pintle, just above the waterline. Using his match he lit the fuse and watched the spark begin its journey.

All this could be done in complete privacy, under the overhang of the stern gallery. To quit the stern, however, was not going to be so easy. Delancey saw with horror that the whole scene was moonlit, the half moon having risen above the cloud belt. There was no choice, though, and he pushed the boat out, telling his two men to pull quietly.

They moved slowly round the port side of the 74 and finally came to rest again under the bowsprit. They must have been seen by now but whoever saw the boat—whether the captain, master or boatswain—must have attributed her presence to someone else's initiative, perhaps cursing himself for not having thought of it. A circuit of inspection was, after all, an obvious precaution. More or less out of sight beneath the bowsprit, Delancey found himself looking up at a formidable figure of Hercules, club in hand. You would look still more disapproving, he thought, if you knew what was about to happen behind you.

Minutes passed, Tanner and Teesdale paddling slowly to prevent the gig being carried shorewards by the tide. The wait seemed endless and Delancey felt that a new plan might be needed. Suppose the fuse had gone out? Dared he go back to relight it? It would be asking too much of his men. But he would have to do something, if only to distract the enemy's attention while his boat rowed away. What was there to do? Could he hit the barrel with a musket shot?

Ten minutes had gone—there was no doubt about that. He had failed again. Looking over towards the other side of the bay, he wondered what Kerr proposed to do. The plan agreed was that he should follow up the *Spitfire*'s attack. Had he turned tail? No, that was unfair. The attack had been a failure and any further attack would be met by the enemy's broadside. It was true that half the 74's starboard guns were masked by the *Spitfire*, but the rest could fire and the French, for that matter, could man the fireship's starboard battery. No, there was little the *Vulture* could do. . . .

At that moment there came an ear-splitting explosion which shook the gig as if she had been hit with a sledge-hammer. It was followed by a babble of sound on board the Frenchman, orders, curses and exclamations. Perhaps, thought Delancey, I have won after all?

'I am going to board the *Spitfire*.' Delancey was almost surprised to hear his own voice say it. There was no doubt in his mind, however, that this was what he must do. As the boat pulled away from the Frenchman's bows he could see a column of smoke rising from the ship's stern. He guessed that her stern-walk would be on fire and possibly her wardroom as well. The fire could almost certainly be put out but the French would have to work hard in the first place to prevent it spreading. He could hear the captain's voice again and could picture the scene on board, with chains of buckets and hatchet men. Their problem would be to save the mizzen mast or what was left of it.

With little risk now of being seen—the French being fully occupied—he took the gig round to the *Spitfire*'s starboard bow. Overhead he could hear the bellowing of orders as the men there were ordered back to their own ship. They were still able to use the *Spitfire*'s foremast as their bridge and he could distinguish the sound as they ran for it. More distantly came the sound of the pumps and the crackle of the flames. There was probably a leak at the Frenchman's sternpost and the water was needed, anyway, for fire-fighting. Or perhaps they were flooding the after-magazine? Whatever they were doing, they would need every man they had.

'Wait here,' Delancey said to his gig's crew, and used a trailing rope to assist his climb into the foremast chains.

His great advantage now lay in his exact knowledge of the ship he had boarded; a ship he had never expected to see again. He knew exactly where everything would be. Making straight for the deserted forecastle, he made a pile there of bedding, canvas, tackle and junk, smashed a scuttle to improve the draught, set a light to the bonfire and then jammed the door on a rope's end. Then he ran aft and repeated the same tactics in a storeroom on the orlop deck. This time he wanted to make certain. It would take ten minutes, he supposed, for the French to realise what was happening, and another ten minutes for the fire to reach the magazine. That would give him time enough to reach the shore at the nearest point. He scrambled once more down the ship's side and into the boat.

'Now, men, pull for your lives!'

Tanner and Teesdale needed no encouragement. There were two more oars in the boat and Delancey took one himself, freed his French prisoner, explained the situation and gave him the fourth.

'Pull like the devil! Pull your guts out! Pull as you never pulled before.'

They were fired upon finally but at long range and quite without effect. It encouraged them, however, to put their backs into it.

'Don't slacken *now*!' Delancey croaked after fifteen minutes. 'Pull!!'

He felt that his lungs would burst, that he was dying for want of a drink, that death from exhaustion was near.

'Pull!' he whispered and the boat was suddenly aground. From the beach came a bellow—it was Fairbrother's voice—

'Surrender, you bastards, or we fire! Come out of that boat with your hands up! Vous êtes prisoniers! Jettez vos armes! Levez les mains! Surrender! . . . Oh, beg pardon, sir. Didn't recognise you. We have a few prisoners here under guard. A pity we didn't burn that French 74, but you had a damned good try, sir. I'll wager she doesn't escape now, not after that last explosion.'

'A still safer bet,—' gasped Delancey, '—after the next.'

From seaward came a detonation like the crack of doom, followed a second later by an explosion which was only fractionally less. Seen clearly in the moonlight, the two ships were blown apart. For some seconds the scene was lit as if by the flames of hell, masts and yards revealed in midair, motionless; then there was a rumble and hissing noise and both ships had gone. The sound of the two explosions re-echoed from across the bay, from the Ox Mountains inland, and then all was silent.

*   *   *

'Now this,' said Captain Kerr, 'is going to be the most extraordinary dispatch I shall ever have to write. I have to describe what will probably be the last fireship attack in the history of warfare. It virtually failed and then you finished the enemy off almost single-handed. I am left speechless—yes, and ashamed.'

'You have no cause to be ashamed, sir.'

'But what am I to say about my own part in the action? The *Vulture* did no more than distract the enemy's attention.'

'You directed the attack, sir, and I merely carried it out. The original failure, moreover, was mine, although I hardly know how the attack could have been improved upon.'

'What do you mean?'

'With so small a target, a single ship's stern, the only way was to have a man at the wheel until the actual collision took place. We could never have hit it otherwise. It was also essential to man the bow chasers so as to return the enemy's fire. Without that our masts and wheel would have gone. But I couldn't set fire to the ship with all those men on board. I left it too late, therefore, and the enemy extinguished the fire. Perhaps the better plan might have been to light a 30-minute fuse to the magazine.'

'But the enemy would have found that. With the ship not ablaze they would have guessed what the trick was. It couldn't have been anything else.'

'Well, sir. I can think of no other plan. Our conclusion must be, I submit, that fireships are of no use save in quite exceptional circumstances. A suitable target does not present itself twice in a lifetime.'

'I am of your opinion about that, captain. I think, however, that the *Spitfire* justified her existence in one way. She has gained you your promotion.'

'Can I be sure of that, sir?'

'As sure as you can be of anything. If destroying a French 74 is not enough, I can't conceive, sir, what more the Admiralty can want.'

'Perhaps they might prefer a man of better family, with more influential relatives.'

'Perhaps they might at that. But listen, Delancey. I shall give you a piece of advice. I come, as you know, of a noble family. When we first met, I thought you a pushing member of the middle class, clever in your way, but no real seaman and not nearly smart enough. I was wrong. You have proved yourself a demon in battle, a far better man than I shall ever be. No, don't interrupt—I recognise that as a fact. It is not your courage I think so remarkable—although you have proved that up to the hilt—but your refusal to accept defeat. Your first plan to destroy the enemy was intelligent and daring but it failed. Ninety-nine officers out of a hundred would have called it a day. They would have said, "I did my best but that bloody ship is still there. I'll leave her to some other confounded hero. What I need is a brandy and a good night's sleep." But you came back again with a new plan, to blow off her damned rudder. And you weren't content even with that. Her rudder gone, you weren't happy until you had blown her to pieces. It is that persistence that sets you apart from the rest.'

'But remember, sir, that we owed our success to two seamen who should not have been there at all. They should have left the *Spitfire* in one of the earlier boats but they hid themselves and stayed aboard with the sole object of helping me escape.'

'I know. I know. You told me. But why should they have cared a damn whether you escaped or not? They had come to believe that your life mattered more than theirs. It is that fact tells me something about your success as a leader. So much for compliments, but I still mean to give you my piece of advice. I have known officers of courage and ability who have lacked family and interest and who have deserved promotion and success. Some of them have come to believe that the world is against them. They have said repeatedly, "I shall never be chosen for any important task" and "There will never be a knighthood for me—all the honours go to men who are well connected." I have known such men say bitter things about men senior to them, about men of flag rank. Some, going further, have affected coarser manners, worse accents than they were born with, as if to prove that a lack of social grace has been the main hindrance to their preferment. But men of this sort are their own worst enemies. Senior officers are not fond of these outspoken critics. Why should they be? By saying "These well-born officers are all against me" an uncouth officer can make it true. So think as well of us as you can. Do not scruple to imitate those little tricks of behaviour which distinguish the man of fashion. Never play the rough tarpaulin in my lady's drawing room. Take my word for it when I tell you that your real abilities will not be overlooked. I am quite confident of your further success, with or without commendation from me or from anyone else. There, I have done. Remember my words, and believe that I sincerely wish you well.'